DETONATE

TIN STAR K9 SERIES

JODI BURNETT

SDG PUBLISHING

DETONATE

PROLOGUE

Nick Morell lifted Livy, his adorable curly-headed, chubby-cheeked, but exhausted Disney princess from the seat on the courtesy van when it pulled to a stop behind their SUV. It had taken fifteen-minutes to load their luggage in the van and drive to the satellite parking from the main terminal at Denver International Airport. He and his wife, Melody, had finally saved enough cash to take their kids on a full week-long vacation to Disney World. It had taken them so long to sock the money away that their son Pete, now twelve, had almost been too "cool" to embrace the magic of the kingdom. Almost. Luckily, within two days, his pre-teen cynicism gave way to wonder, and their family trip became everything Nick and Melody had hoped for.

The sky was an inky black when they landed at DIA. Gathering everyone's stuff together, they had trudged off the plane, up the jetway, and made their way to the underground train that transported them to the main terminal. At baggage claim, it seemed to take hours before their luggage finally flopped onto the circulating belt, and their tired kids got cranky.

After a giant yawn, Nick had worried he'd be too tired to drive home, but the minute they stepped outside, he sucked in a breath of the pure, crisp Colorado air he preferred—a nice break from the water-clogged inhales he'd endured in the humid climate of Florida—and he was momentarily rejuvenated.

Nick's whole family was already worn out from the week's worth of adventure, and the prospect of the long car ride home made it worse. They still had another hour to drive before they could all collapse on their own beds. Stifling a second yawn, he pulled the remaining few dollars from his wallet to tip their shuttle driver.

"Thanks again for driving us all the way to our car. I really appreciate not having to walk from the bus stop to the end of the parking lot with all this stuff."

"It's my pleasure," the man answered in an accent Nick didn't recognize. "Besides, it's late and I have no other passengers, so it's no problem." The driver accepted the tip and gave Nick a little bow. "Thank you, sir."

He proceeded to unload the luggage from the back of the small bus while Nick unlocked the car. He strapped his four-year-old daughter into her car seat, making sure the five-point safety harness was snug. "There you go, Princess Jasmine."

"I'm not Jasmine, Daddy. I'm Cinderella." Livy's pudgy fists rubbed her tired blue eyes as she snuggled against the seat and drifted back to sleep. Nick chuckled. His daughter had on clear plastic shoes that resembled Cinderella's glass slippers, a yellow dress designed to look like Belle's ballgown, and a sea-green and gold tiara that emulated Jasmine's crowning glory. An aqua and white rubberized medallion rested on her small chest that was a copy of the heart of Te Fiti that Moana wore. Livy believed with all her heart she was the perfect combination of all the heroine princesses. How was he to know which one she was in her imagination at any given moment?

He kissed the soft blonde curls on the top of her head and went to help his wife load the luggage into the back of their SUV. Equally sleepy as his little sister, Pete struggled with his suitcase. Nick, filled with a sense of pride and deep satisfaction, ruffled his son's straight brown hair. "Hey, bud, I appreciate you helping, but why don't you get in the car with your sister? Mom and I will take care of the bags."

He smiled at Melody. His wife's wild blonde ringlets were an exact match to their daughter's. He pushed a stray curl behind her ear, his fingers lingering on her cheek. "Well, we did it, Mel. The perfect family vacation."

Melody gave him a weary but genuine smile. "We sure did. We've certainly made some lifelong memories." She reached for his hand and squeezed. "Thanks, Nick. You worked so hard to make this trip happen. You're a great dad, you know that?"

Nick's chest swelled, and he leaned forward to kiss her. "We both worked hard, and it couldn't have been more perfect. It was everything we hoped for." He scooted his wife toward the front passenger door. "Get in, Honey. I'll finish packing up and then we can head for home.

Honestly, I can't wait to crawl into our bed when we get there."

He returned to the back of the car and waved at the van driver as the man began to pull away. Nick's brain vaguely registered the sound of a click. A fraction of a breath later, a white light radiated from an electrical box attached to the lamppost in front of the SUV. The intensity blinded him, searing his eyes. The painful blaze flared larger and brighter, bringing with it unimaginable heat. Nick's skin seemed to melt from his bones. His mind flew through his life experiences, vainly racking itself to make sense of what was happening. A searing gale-force blast lifted him off his feet, shattering him into a million pieces and scattering his essence into the eternal night. His last conscious thought was of his family.

HYPER-SENSITIZED NERVES MIMICKED the billowing explosion that lit up the night sky and skittered like fire up his spinal column, down through the ends of the bomber's fingers and toes, and up through his scalp. His body lightened with a glowing sense of accomplishment. He was euphoric and giddy with excitement. "Awesome!" he murmured as he marveled at the slowly dimming brilliance and tapped the start button on his watch's timer. He stared in wonder from their perch at the top of the landfill northwest of DIA at the explosion and its aftermath. The result of their experiment hovered and brightened the dark night over the abandoned long-term parking lot.

"Now, let's see how long it takes for emergency services to respond." Ignoring the rotten fruit and sweaty-shoe stench of the garbage dump, he uncovered the lenses of his binoculars and watched the events unfold now that the intense lumens had decreased enough for him to observe without being blinded. "I wish we could have watched close up." He adjusted the lenses. "Looks like we took out a total of three vehicles."

"I didn't think such a small device could be that effective. There's no way anyone within a twenty-mile radius could miss that beauty! It was better than the 4th of July fireworks," his partner exclaimed. "People had to see it. As far away as the airport is from that parking lot, I bet it still only takes the cops less than five minutes to get there."

He scoffed. "Even at top speed, they'll take longer than that. Remember, first they have to receive a reporting call. Then there will be several seconds of coordination before they deploy the police, fire, and ambulance."

"I wonder how long it will take for them to realize this is more than an electrical box gone bad."

"We'll get to hear all about it on the news." He grinned. "Monitoring this and the few other events we have planned as they play out will give us all the information we need to accomplish our magnum opus."

1

Caitlyn nudged her husband's wool-sock encased foot with her own as they snuggled together on their leather couch with their feet propped up on the coffee table while they enjoyed their first early morning fire of the season. The comforting warmth of the golden flames seeped into her soles. Renegade, her Belgian Malinois K9 partner and best friend, lay stretched out on the hearthrug soaking the heat into his russet and black fur. Autumn had come early to Moose Creek, Wyoming, and the air outside was as crisp as the falling leaves. Caitlyn burrowed under a log cabin quilt as the rays of dawn beamed in through the windows, promising a beautiful fall day.

Colt rested his hand on her still-flat belly. "How are you feeling today?"

"I think my morning sickness is finally in the past. And I'll tell you what, I sure will be glad when I can drink regular coffee again." She raised her mug. "This decaf just isn't the same." She swung her feet around and tucked them underneath her hip before she took another sip.

A grin lit her husband's ruggedly handsome face. His dark blond morning whiskers, still unshaven, gave a rough edge to his square jaw. "It's so hard for me to imagine having a little baby living here with us. Where are we going to put all his stuff?"

Caitlyn glanced around their cozy living room. It was true. Their cabin was getting too small. They'd already converted a storage closet into a tiny bedroom for Colt's son, Jace. It worked for the nights when he stayed with them. "You don't know if the baby is a him or a her." She nudged Colt's ribs playfully. "Besides, babies don't take up much room." Her tone was unconvincing, even to her own ears.

"Have you seen the tons of stuff Dylan and McKenzie have spread all over your parents' house? Cribs, playpens, swings... And we don't have a tenth of the space they do."

Caitlyn giggled. "Yeah, but my brother and his wife don't even use half of that junk. Don't worry, the baby will sleep in our room for the first couple of months, and then we'll figure it out. In the olden days, whole families lived together in one-room cabins."

Colt's brows crunched together, and he turned to look at her full on. "No privacy. I'm not liking that idea. And what will we do when the baby needs *his* own space?"

She sighed. "I don't know. Do you think we could build an addition? I love this place, and I really don't want to move, but you're right. She will need a room of her own."

"I'll talk to your dad. He'll know what changes we

could realistically make. We might be able to add on a room, but there's no way that can happen until next summer. I'm concerned about what we're going to do until then?"

Caitlyn's phone rang, saving her from having to come up with a viable plan. The caller ID said, US Government. "Hello? This is Deputy US Marshal Reed." She sat forward to take the call.

"Reed. Commander Dutton here. Have you seen the news yet this morning?"

"No, sir." She reached for the TV remote, hoping to catch up on whatever breaking news had caused the Spec. Ops Commander to call her so early. "What happened?"

"A bomb went off last night at a parking lot near Denver International Airport."

An icy chill sent a rash of goosebumps rising across her skin. "Was anyone hurt?"

"Unfortunately, yes. A family of four and a courtesy van driver were all killed."

The TV screen brightened the darkened room, stealing with it the cozy atmosphere she'd been enjoying with Colt. Caitlyn switched the channel to the news and took in live images of a burn scar at the edge of a parking lot. With lights flashing, cop cars and fire engines surrounded three burned-out vehicles. "Any idea who's responsible?"

"Not yet. So far, no one is claiming responsibility. The event was five miles away from the airport, but the FBI is taking no chances. They're investigating it as an act of terror and have been tasked with searching the entire property for secondary devices."

"Is that why you're calling me?"

"Yes. I know you're on light duty these days, but I'd like you to consider joining a combined task force of federal K9 agents, including the FBI, ATF, and Homeland teams, along with local K9 cops, to help search the property. The FBI needs all hands on deck and reached out to our Special Operations Group. I'm sending out four K9 teams from the SOG Unit, and since you live close to DIA, I thought you might join them. That airport covers 53 square miles. It's an enormous undertaking."

"My brother is an FBI K9 handler for the Denver Bomb Unit. He's probably involved in the case."

"Yes, I saw that in your file. I'm certain he is. So, you'll go?"

"Of course." Caitlyn risked a peek at Colt and received the glower she expected. "Let me know when and where, and I'll be there." She offered her husband a wobbly smile.

Colt shoved the quilt aside and crossed his arms over his chest. When she ended the call, his eyes blazed with accusation. "We had an agreement, Catie."

"I know, but I won't be chasing bad guys. All this job involves is an explosive materials search. There's a ton of ground to cover at DIA, and they need all the help they can get."

"What about the baby? You promised you would stay out of harm's way until he's born."

"You're right, but this really isn't as dangerous as it sounds. If a dog finds something, then we back off and call in the bomb unit. They're the ones taking the risks." Caitlyn took hold of Colt's hands, pulling his arms away from his chest. "Besides, this will give me one last chance to work before I get too huge to do anything. And Logan will be there. You know he'll keep an eye on me." She hoped she could convince her husband to see reason.

"I'll say it straight out, Caitlyn. I don't want you to go." His hazel eyes glinted in the glow of the fire like shards of broken sea glass.

"Why don't you call Logan? He can explain the mission, and besides, the explosion came from a small device. Nothing professional. It was probably a one-time thing. A prank. I'll just be helping make certain of that."

"Why can't you sit still for six more months? Why is it you insist on putting yourself in danger?"

"Said the pot to the kettle." She grasped one of his hands in hers. "Listen, I promise I'll be careful. I just want to help. Besides, it isn't *me* who loves danger. How do you think Logan feels? He finds the bombs, but it's *his* wife who's the adrenaline junkie. Addison is the one who climbs into the bomb suit and dismantles these things."

"Is that supposed to make me feel better?"

"Think of this as a field exercise. It will help keep Renegade's skills sharp." At the mention of his name, Ren hopped up from the floor and moved to sit next to Caitlyn. He rested his chin on her thigh and she stroked his sleek head.

"I don't know." Colt sighed and sounded like he was wavering.

"Colt, we both have potentially dangerous jobs. We knew that when we got married. I want to do this. I promise I'll stay safe, and when I get home, it'll be a full year before I'm able to do any work besides paper shuffling. I *need* to do this." She pleaded with her eyes.

Colt stood, and leaving her on the couch, walked toward their bedroom. "You know how I feel about it—as if that matters." He tossed the words over his shoulder and disappeared through the door.

2

Thunder sounded outside and shook the walls of their hundred-and-twenty-year-old house in downtown Denver. Rain beat a constant tattoo against the wavy antique glass windows as Logan moved up behind his wife, gripping her silk-robed shoulders. Addison scrambled eggs at their ancient gas stove as he pressed up against her. He brushed aside her short black curls so he could kiss the side of her delicate pale neck.

"It's the perfect morning to go back to bed, don't you think? What do you say about being an hour or so late to work?" Logan's bomb-sniffing Belgian Malinois, Gunner, had padded after him into the kitchen and sat at their feet. He cocked his head to the side as if wondering what Addison would think of his partner's plan.

Addison turned to face Logan and gave his chest a little push. "Not today, cowboy. I just got a call about the explosion we saw on the news. Sanchez is holding a briefing at HQ first thing this morning. He's putting together a joint task force to investigate the incident."

"Already? That seems like overkill for a homemade bomb that only took out three cars."

"Three vehicles and five innocent people." Addison's shoulders drooped. "A family of four and a van driver."

Logan stepped back, drawing his brows together. "There was no mention of victims on the news."

"I doubt the reporters knew it at the time. Unfortunately, there was a family of four and a courtesy van driver who were caught in the blast." Logan said nothing to that, his heart thudding heavily as he imagined the horrible loss of life made more tragic knowing two of the victims were kids.

"Sanchez must have a reason to suspect more to the incident than we know, or he wouldn't have called in the troops."

"I guess we'll find out when we get there." Logan's initial plan had been to tease Addy back into bed by reminding her that, as his boss, she could excuse them both for a late show. In light of the tragedy, though, he lost his impetus. "I'll make us some toast."

LOGAN AND GUNNER followed Addison into the briefing room at FBI Headquarters. Special Agent in Charge Rick Sanchez stood in a suit behind a podium at the front of the room, which contained three rows of long tables under bright florescent lighting. He'd pulled his tie loose and unbuttoned the neck of his shirt. Sanchez looked like he'd been at headquarters all night.

Small groups representing the various federal agencies hovered around the edges of the room. Most agents sipped steaming coffee from paper cups. Similarly, Logan, Gunner, and Addy joined a handful of Denver FBI agents who had claimed the front right corner. Standing with them were two other K9 handlers, Clay Jennings and Kendra Dean. Clay and Kendra's dogs weren't with them, and Logan figured their partners were waiting for them out at the FBI K9 facility.

Logan acknowledged a couple of ATF dog handlers whom he recognized from missions they'd previously run together. The agents returned his nod from the other side of the room. Presumably, the third group milling around at the back—none of whom Logan had met before— were from Homeland Security. Four US Marshals suited up in tactical gear leaned against the back wall presumably representing their division.

SAC Sanchez brought the meeting to order. "Everyone, please take a seat." He waited for the agents to comply before he continued. "I'm sure you all have heard the news about the bomb that went off in a satellite parking lot at Denver International Airport last night. Forensic specialists from the Colorado Bureau of Investigation are currently examining the evidence gathered at the scene. Most of you in this room have been called in to assist in what will be a vast search of the DIA property to find any possible secondary devices. We have no specific indication that there are any, but obviously, we need to be certain."

Logan's phone buzzed in his pocket, and he glanced at his smartwatch to see who was texting him. His little sister's nickname appeared on the screen along with her text message.

> Catie-did: Hey Log, I'm headed down to Denver today to join the task force searching for explosives at DIA. U on the case too?

Logan pulled his phone from the cargo pocket on the side of his pants to respond:

> Yeah. In a briefing now. What's your ETA?

> Catie-did: Tonight 7ish

> Logan: Come straight to the house. You can stay with us.

> Catie-did: Thanks. I was hoping you would offer. Looking forward to working with you and Gunner!

Logan held the text stream up so Addison could read it. She smiled with a nod and whispered, "It'll be good to have Caitlyn and Renegade's help."

"Yeah, but do you think she should she be working? She's pregnant, you know."

Addison's eyes narrowed slightly, and Logan braced himself for her ire at his male perspective. "Your sister is a smart and capable woman. I'm sure she can make that decision for herself."

Logan shrugged, but he wondered how Colt felt about Caitlyn doing fieldwork. Logan sure as hell wouldn't want Addison to be on the job if she were pregnant. He sighed. He and Addy had agreed they would like to have kids someday, but now he wondered how *they* would handle the dangerous aspects of their work in the context of having a family. Addison's expertise might ultimately get in the way of them having children.

Sanchez continued. "Hopefully, the rain will clear up soon. I know the weather conditions make it harder for the dogs, but I have faith in them and in you." He passed the mechanics of the search off to his right-hand man, Burke Cameron.

Agent Cameron stepped up to the podium and rested his iPad on it. He typed on the screen and an image of the explosion's aftermath was casted from the device onto the smart board that hung on the wall at the front of the room. "As you know, three vehicles were involved in the incident, and five people lost their lives. Someone attached a bomb to an electrical box in the parking lot next to the parked cars. At this time, we do not know if any of the victims were specifically targeted, or if they simply happened to be in the wrong place at the wrong time."

One of the ATF agents interrupted. "What intel do you have on the parents and the van driver? Where did they work? What was their ideology? Their religion or political affiliation?"

Cameron nodded in response to the questions. "Mr. Morell was in finance at a small firm in Parker. Mrs. Morell was a stay-at-home mom. As far as we can determine, the family went to the local Lutheran church and were likely politically conservative. We know this only through our initial search of their social media accounts and interviews with friends and neighbors. But neither Mr. nor Mrs. Morell posted many political opinions, so it's hard to tell for certain this early in our investigation. We are still searching for solid information on the van driver. I'll get back to you with any new information as it becomes available."

"Burke," Addison raised a hand to gain Cameron's attention. "Has anyone claimed responsibility for the bombing?"

"No, ma'am. Not yet. We'll keep you up to date on that as well as new information as it comes in." Cameron turned back to the rest of the room. "We know very little at this point, but several high-level politicians are flying into Denver next week, and we want to be sure they'll be safe when they get here."

After several more questions, Burke concluded the meeting and handed out the assignments. On their way out of the room, Clay, who was the head of the Denver K9 Unit, nudged Logan's arm. "I hear your sister is coming down as one of the Marshals joining the task force."

"Yeah, she texted me a few minutes ago."

"Outstanding. I look forward to working with her. I've been wanting to talk to her about future Renegade puppies, anyway. So, this is convenient."

Logan bobbed his head. "She's getting in tonight."

"Good. How's Gunner doing?" Clay reached down to scratch the underside of Gunner's chin and received a friendly lick in return. It had been Clay who had given Gunner his initial training before Logan joined the

Denver FBI K9 team and he'd had to work hard to gain his new commander's trust and respect. He was greatly honored when Clay offered to let him work with Gunner. "He's awesome. Eager to get to work."

"All the dogs will be happy to be out in the field. We'll see how well they do with all this rain."

3

____

Colt angrily rubbed his wet hair with a towel while Caitlyn filled a canvas travel bag with clothes for her trip. Swallowing his irritation, he dressed quickly and went to wake Jace. Light from the doorway draped over his son's bed, revealing the boy, sleeping face down, with his lanky body spread at an angle across the twin mattress. One of his legs hung off the edge, and all the covers lay pooled on the floor.

"Hey, kiddo, time to rise and shine."

Jace rolled away from the brightness streaming in through his bedroom door, so Colt turned on the overhead light. "Come on, sleepyhead. You need to eat a solid breakfast before the bus gets here."

"I don't wanna go to school," Jace groaned and buried his head under his pillow. Stretching, his son's gray pit bull, Storm, pressed up from his sleeping spot next to the bed and licked the back of Jace's neck and his bare arm. Jace flapped his hand around blindly until he found Storm and stroked his head.

Colt chuckled. "So, what else is new? Come on. Get up." Leaving the light on, Colt strode to the kitchen to start breakfast. He pulled some fresh blueberries from the refrigerator and started a pot of water to make oatmeal.

Caitlyn rounded the corner with their empty coffee mugs in hand. "Want more?"

"Always." He smiled, not wanting their earlier conversation to turn into an argument. But he still wanted her to understand where he was coming from. "You know, Catie, I'm really proud of how dedicated you are to your work. You and Renegade make an amazing law-enforcement team. And I know you love your job. But what about the fact that you are now also a mother? It doesn't seem like you took that into consideration when you said yes to going to Denver."

His wife set the coffee cups down carefully before turning to eye him speculatively. "Don't you think I have the same dedication to being a mom as I do to my work?"

"I'm sure you will when our baby is born, but you're carrying him right now. Not to mention, you help care for Jace when he's here. He needs you too, you know. He's just started middle school, and lately he has this whole new pre-teen attitude I don't know what to do with. I really want us to be together as we raise our kids. That's all. Do you think that's unreasonable?"

"It sounds like you want me to be a stay-at-home mom, which is never something we've discussed. You know I want to maintain my career *and* be a mom, right? So, yeah, in a way, I think you're being unreasonable."

"I know you want to keep working, but things are

changing with Jace. Lately, all he wants is independence from me and Allison. He thinks he should be able to make all his own decisions. He's already struggling in school, even though the semester just started a few weeks ago. I'm worried about him."

Jace trudged into the room followed by his dog, effectively ending their conversation. Storm and Renegade greeted each other with sniffs and playful mouthing. Jace had put on his clothes, but the jeans he chose were dirty, his hair stood on end, and his eyes were still droopy. "I don't know why I have to go to school at all. I already know what I want to be when I grow up, and I don't have to go to college to do it. I should just drop out of school."

Caitlyn poured coffee—Colt's from the pot and hers from the Keurig—into the two mugs and handed Colt his. She blew on hers before asking, "What is it you want to be?"

Jace brightened a little. "I'm going to be a cowboy, just like Uncle Dylan!"

Caitlyn smiled as she sipped her coffee. She reached out to smooth her stepson's messy hair. "He'll love hearing that. You should talk to Dylan about what it takes to become a cattle rancher. Did you know he has a degree in agriculture from Colorado State University?"

Jace slumped into a chair at the table with a dejected air. "No."

Colt winked at Caitlyn. "There's a lot to learn if you want to be a successful rancher like your uncle and Grandpa John. And I bet they'd love to talk to you about it—*after* school." He ladled oatmeal into three bowls and topped the hot cereal off with berries, milk, and honey.

"One of the first things they'd tell you is you have to get up way before dawn to tend to the animals. No sleeping in on a ranch. Not even on the weekends or holidays." Colt set a bowl before his son. "Here, eat up. The bus will be here in ten minutes."

JACE PLUNGED a spoon into his breakfast. He didn't want to hear why he couldn't follow his dreams, or why he should go to school, or worse, go to college. Blah, blah, blah. All he wanted was to ride the range with his uncle. Besides, if he lived on the ranch, he wouldn't cause problems between his dad and mom, and his dad wouldn't ask Caitlyn to stay home to babysit him. He knew she didn't want to do that. She loved *her* job, too.

Jace worried about what things were going to be like when the new baby was born. His dad and Caitlyn probably wouldn't want him around anymore. But if he stayed out at the ranch, he could run the property with his uncle, he could earn his own keep, and he'd be out of everyone's way. There were lots of empty bedrooms at his grandparents' house and if he lived there, his dad wouldn't have to build onto the cabin.

Sighing, he took another bite of the hot cereal. The cool berries popped open with a burst of sweet juice but that didn't interrupt the path of his thoughts. His mom, of course, would *never* agree to let him live out at the ranch. But somehow, he had to find a way. Lately, his mom had been talking about moving them back to Missouri, and Jace couldn't let that happen. He would be miserable without his dad and Caitlyn and the ranch. And what about his dog and his horse? He'd have to leave Rusty at the ranch, and his mom would never let him bring Storm with them. She didn't even let him bring his dog to her house when it was her parenting time. He'd miss everything that was important to him if his mom made him move to another state. Frustrated, Jace shoved his half-eaten bowl away. His stomach cramped as he went to grab his backpack.

"Hey!" His dad's brows wrinkled together, making his face look stern. "What kind of manners are those? If you're finished, which you are not, you can take your bowl to the sink."

"I'm not hungry." Jace wanted to stalk away, but he knew better than to be disrespectful to his dad, so he grabbed the bowl and plunked it down in the sink.

"What's gotten into you?"

"Nothing." Jace sidestepped his dad and strode down the hall to his room.

A few minutes later, Caitlyn knocked on his door, then opened it. "Hey, kiddo. Are you okay?"

Jace shrugged. He was not okay, but he didn't want to talk about it. Caitlyn couldn't do anything to change things, anyway.

"I thought maybe Ren and I could walk you out to the bus stop. I'm leaving today and won't be back for a few days. I want to spend as much time with you now as I can."

"Sure, I guess." He'd miss Caitlyn when she was gone. She never pressured him.

"I bet Storm would like to come, too."

"Whatever." Jace did his best to sound like he didn't care, but he couldn't resist rubbing Storm's velvety head on his way to the bathroom to brush his teeth.

Jace let his dad hug him on his way out the door. He even stood still when his dad kissed the top of his head, though it made him want to squirm. Kissing was for babies.

"Have a good day, son. We can talk more about your future over dinner tonight. How about we go out to the café? Just us guys?"

"I guess." Jace said with as little enthusiasm as possible. He wanted his dad to know how unhappy he was without having to say it.

Caitlyn and the dogs followed Jace out of the cabin and down the front steps. They walked halfway down the long drive before she said, "I bet you wish you could make all your own decisions about school and life, huh?"

Jace peered up at her and took several steps before he answered. "Yeah. I mean, it's *my* life, right?"

"That's true. And I know you want to be a cowboy, but there is a lot more to being an adult than just having a job... even if it's your dream job. There's a lot to learn."

"Like what?"

"Like how to manage your life as an adult."

"What do you mean?" He peered up at her out of the side of his eye.

"Well, you need to know what foods to eat so you can stay healthy. You need to understand basic math so you can pay your bills or buy anything that involves payments, like a house or a truck."

"All of that is boring. Besides, I could figure all that out."

"You probably could, but it's easier with an education."

"Did you go to college?"

She gave him a crooked grin. "Twice."

Jace stopped walking and stared up at her. "Twice? Why?" That sounded like torture to him.

She laughed. Jace liked Caitlyn's laugh—how her nose wrinkled, and her face turned soft and bright when she smiled. "Because the first time I went, I didn't have any goals. I didn't know what I wanted to study, and to be honest, I didn't try very hard. The second time, I worked harder and got my degree in Criminal Justice."

"And then you became a deputy marshal?"

"After some experience as a sheriff's deputy, yep." They started walking again. "And you're already doing far better than I was at eighteen because you know what you want to do. Either way, school is important. Education helps you have a more successful life, no matter what you want to become. Not everyone has to go to college, but it's smart to graduate from high school."

"I guess." He didn't really agree, but he didn't want to disappoint Caitlyn with his true feelings on the matter. They stopped at the road and waited as the yellow bus rumbled toward them.

"I won't embarrass you by giving you a big hug and sloppy kiss in front of your friends, but imagine that I did, because I want to." Caitlyn laughed and squeezed him from the side. "I'll see you in a couple of days. I'll miss you."

He tried but couldn't keep the smile off his lips. "Me too." He looked away and patted the dogs.

"I won't get into Denver until late tonight, but I'll call you tomorrow, okay?"

Jace didn't say so, but he wasn't planning on being home when she called.

4

Caitlyn left for Denver as soon as she and the dogs returned to the cabin from walking Jace to the bus. Colt's displeasure with her decision regarding the assignment was palpable, but she simply couldn't miss the opportunity to work with Logan. No matter what her own accomplishments had been, Logan would always be her greatest hero. It was her brother who got her interested in K9 work in the first place. Of course, Commander Dutton's phone call wanting to keep her engaged with the SOG unit was a much-needed ego boost after a month of boring paperwork.

Sitting at a desk staring at the computer was going to make for a tedious nine months combined with the six weeks of maternity leave after her baby was born. Caitlyn didn't know how she'd stand it. She and Renegade were meant for high-action fieldwork, not sedentary web-surfing. Her poor dog was going to go stir-crazy.

As though he sensed her agitation, Renegade poked his nose through the opening between the kennel in the back of Caitlyn's specially fitted K9 vehicle and the driver's seat. He licked the side of her face. She laughed and looped her arm under his chin, hugging him to her cheek. Renegade was the best dog in the world, as far as she was concerned, and they were going to have one last hurrah before they were stuck at home being pregnant.

It was a six-hour drive down to Denver from Moose Creek alone, but Caitlyn had promised to swing by the US Marshal's Office in Casper to check in, which added another hour or so to their journey. The length of the trip depended on the duration of her meeting with her local boss, Chief Deputy Keith Spencer.

He wanted to discuss her role in the office during her pregnancy, and Caitlyn planned to bring up Chief Deputy Grey's offer for her to work jointly from the Casper office and the Marshals office up in Billings. Caitlyn was eager to convince Spencer that it was efficient for her and Renegade to split their efforts between the two small offices. If she couldn't remain deployed with SOG, she'd like to stay busy with work from both field offices.

By the time they arrived in Casper, Caitlyn was so ravenous her belly hurt. The intense hunger she experienced these days was going to take some getting used to. Every four hours, her body acted as if she was starving to death. Her stomach rolled and contracted in on itself. She absolutely *had* to get lunch right then, before she met Chief Spencer at his office. There was no option, even if it made her late.

She and Renegade turned into a drive-through barbecue restaurant where she knew they would give

Renegade a small bowl of pulled pork without sauce. Caitlyn ordered a large combo platter with pork, corn, coleslaw, mashed potatoes with gravy and an extra piece of cornbread. With the enticing aroma of the food filling her car, she barely parked before diving into the meal. She and Renegade sat in the parking lot polishing off their feast.

Caitlyn was still licking tangy barbecue sauce from her fingers when she and Ren entered the US Marshals Casper Office. She waved at two deputies she knew and bobbed her head in acknowledgement of several unfamiliar faces before she knocked at the chief's office.

"Enter!"

She pushed the door open, and Renegade followed her through. "Hi, Chief. Sorry if I'm a little late. I had to get something to eat."

Keith Spencer, a slightly balding man in his fifties, chuckled and gestured for her to take a seat in front of his desk. "Yeah, I remember when my wife was pregnant with our three. I used to tease that I had to push food toward her with a long stick because I was afraid if I offered my hand I'd draw back a bloody stump."

Caitlyn grinned. "The level of hunger is no joke, sir."

"So, you're on your way down to Denver to assist in the efforts there in the aftermath of the explosion at DIA?"

"Yes, sir. I know it will be a long while before I can return to active duty after this assignment, so I accepted the mission from SOG."

"We are preparing to keep you busy with computer work here over the next several months. I know the guys are looking forward to having more tech support and help with their paperwork and digital research."

Caitlyn's heart withered. "I don't like the idea of becoming their personal admin, sir. But I will make myself content with assisting in data searches that'll help apprehend our most wanted criminals until Renegade and I can get back out and start hunting them down ourselves."

"I figured you'd feel that way, but I know you'll give this office whatever support we need while you're on light duty."

A disappointed gust of air rushed from Caitlyn's lungs. "Yes, sir." Renegade, whose eyes never left her, let out a tiny whine commiserating with her aggravation. "While we're on the topic of light-duty, I wanted to ask you if you'd had a chance to discuss the idea of my splitting time between this office and the Marshals office in Billings with Chief Grey?"

"Yes, Chief Grey and I had a long conversation about the feasibility of that plan. The sticking point is, of course, payroll budgets and so forth. Especially since we are not in the same regions." Caitlyn forced her shoulders to remain straight as she braced for Spencer to reject the idea. "But I believe we'll work things out by the time you and Renegade are ready to return to full duty after your maternity leave."

"So, not before then?"

"No, the Billings office already has an admin who manages their office, so your working for them would be redundant. Our deputies here need your assistance at this time. I'm sure you're fine with that decision, aren't you, Reed?"

Caitlyn gave herself an internal shrug. She supposed it didn't really make a difference. She was going to be stuck doing computer work whether it was here or there, so she might as well get used to it. "Yes, sir. And I appreciate the opportunity to work for both offices when Ren and I are back on the job next spring."

"Good. That's settled then. I know you're eager to get on the road to Denver, so I'll let you get on your way. Expect a desk-load of work waiting for you next week. I'm happy to allow you to do the bulk of it from home, but I expect you to be present in this office a minimum of one day a week for the duration. Is that clear?"

"Yes, sir. Thank you." Caitlyn and Renegade left his office and spent a few brief minutes saying hello to her fellow deputies before they got back into her Explorer and headed south on I-25.

It was almost dinnertime when Caitlyn parked on the curb in front of Logan and his wife Addison's vintage home in downtown Denver. Logan bolted out the front door and jumped down the steps toward her car, followed by his dog, Gunner. Addison stepped out of the house but remained on the porch, holding the door open and waving.

"Hey, Catie-did! It's great to see you! You look... well... you're glowing!" He hugged her tight and lifting her, spun her in a circle before reaching into the car and pushing the kennel release button so that Renegade could get out and play with Gunner in the front yard. Keeping an arm around her shoulders, her brother took her bag from her and walked her up to the porch.

Addison pulled her into a giant hug. "I'm so glad you're here, and I'm looking forward to working with you and Ren. We need all the K9 noses we can get on this case. ATF is already on site. FBI Headquarters has tasked us to join them in searching the entire DIA property to be certain there are no other explosives anywhere."

"I'm excited to be here. I've always wanted to work with Logan—you know—show him how it's done, and all." Caitlyn laughed as Logan gave her a gentle shove.

"Right." He rolled his eyes skyward. "Who was it that taught you everything you know, again?"

Caitlyn pushed her brother back. "Sure, you taught me in the beginning, but the student has surpassed the master!"

"Yeah, yeah. So, you say. We'll see." Logan stood back to let her enter the house and followed behind Addison with both dogs in tow. "Dinner is just about ready. I'll show you where the bathroom is and where you're going to sleep." He led the way upstairs and set her bag on an old-style wrought iron bed in a small room with a sloping ceiling. "Bathroom's down the hall."

After Caitlyn freshened up from the long drive and fed Ren his supper, she, Logan, and Addison sat down for their meal. Before Logan shoveled a forkful of pasta dripping with marinara into his mouth, he said, "We're so happy for you and Colt about the baby, Caitlyn." He chewed the giant bite and swallowed. "How does Colt feel about you working this case?"

Caitlyn's shoulders drooped as she let out a long sigh. "Way to wreck my appetite, you big jerk."

"That well, huh?"

"Let's say he isn't thrilled. But he supports me. It's going to be a long time before I'll be back at work after this. I think, deep down, he understands that."

Addison reached for Caitlyn's hand and gave it a squeeze. "Just be careful, okay? We'd hate for anything bad to happen on our watch."

"I will, but *you* understand, don't you, Addy? I mean, as a female agent, and all?"

"Sure, I do. But *I'm* not pregnant. You have a bigger responsibility now, you know?"

5

The next morning, Logan and Gunner entered the briefing room at the FBI Headquarters building, followed by his wife and his sister with Renegade. Special Agent in Charge Rick Sanchez stood at the front preparing to begin the meeting, which involved team leaders from the FBI, ATF, Homeland Security, and the US Marshals. Logan led the way over to the FBI K9 contingent and nodded at Clay Jennings, the former US Marine who was now the K9 Unit Commander. Only Logan and Caitlyn had their dogs with them.

"Where's your partner?" Logan asked as he shook Jennings's hand.

Clay stood an easy six-foot-four and towered over Logan's six-foot frame. "Ranger and Annie are waiting for us at the unit kennels. Dean and I will pick them up on our way out to the airport." Clay smiled at Caitlyn. "Hey, junior Reed. Good to see you." He clasped her hand and then reached down to pet Renegade. "Hi Ren. Good boy. You gonna help us out today, buddy?" Clay introduced

Caitlyn to Kendra Dean. The petite, but athletically built, K9 agent wore her dark hair pulled back into a high ponytail she threaded through the back of a navy-blue baseball cap with the letters FBI K9 emblazoned in bright white across the front.

SAC Sanchez addressed the room and brought them all to attention. "Thank you all for being here this morning. We've had teams working through the night, and so far, they've found no other explosives. We will all pitch in on this effort, but our leads will be the various K9 units. We're covering a vast area as we search the entire DIA property, which covers approximately 34,000 acres. Dogs and bomb squads from the ATF, Homeland, the Marshals, along with local law enforcement personnel will canvas all parking facilities and building sites open to public traffic, searching for secondary explosives. Meanwhile, we'll investigate potential suspects and determine possible motives for the bombing and hopefully determine whether the incident has anything to do with the upcoming political summit scheduled for next week.

"The federal government is compiling a list of attendees expected to arrive in Denver for the conclave. We currently have agents scouring the wires for chatter about the explosion. Let's hope it was just a random act rather than a precursor to a terror event, but either way we must find the culprit before more damage is done. After our search of DIA, we will expand our explosive material sweeps to the summit's conference center, to be on the safe side.

"Colorado Bureau of Investigation is currently testing the evidence we gathered at the explosion site and will soon let us know exactly what we're dealing with. Hopefully, we'll have enough evidence to track down the bomber and make an arrest."

Sanchez assigned the various teams to their search locations, and as soon as Clay had the information for his unit, Logan and the rest of the K9 officers followed him out of the room. Remaining professional, Logan subtly squeezed Addison's hand as he passed by her and murmured. "Stay safe out there today." He followed the example Sanchez set, who was married to Agent Dean. They rarely, if ever, showed any public displays of affection at work.

"You do the same." Addison's eyes met his with meaning, and he bobbed his head before releasing her fingers.

His sister didn't share his reserve and gave Addison a hug before she followed him out to his car. Both their dogs loaded up into the K9 kennel in the back of his specially outfitted Explorer. They easily shared the space since they were already friends. Logan drove Caitlyn and the dogs out to the FBI K9 Unit at the edge of the city to get their assignments from Clay.

They joined Clay and Kendra inside the unit building after those two had retrieved their dogs from the yard. Clay's Belgian was bigger than the other dogs and looked like a solid-black wolf. The sweet-faced chocolate Lab belonged to Kendra and was known for her acute nose. Logan had worked explosive searches with both of them before and was confident in their excellent capabilities. Three other FBI K9 agents joined them, adding another Belgian Malinois, a Belgian Shepherd, and a black Lab to the mix.

Kendra leaned close to Caitlyn and murmured, "You may not remember, but we met at Logan and Addison's wedding."

"I recall." Caitlyn smiled. "It's good to see you again, Kendra. I'm looking forward to working with you. I rarely get to hang out with other female handlers."

"Same here." She held her fingers out for Ren to sniff. "I thought Renegade was an apprehension and attack dog?"

Caitlyn laughed. "He is, but he's a multipurpose dog, thanks to Logan."

Logan shrugged. "Guilty as charged. I was home in Wyoming between my time in the Army and the FBI Academy when Caitlyn adopted Renegade. So, I helped her train him. Cait didn't have any idea she wanted to go into law enforcement at the time, so there was no need to specialize his training. Truth is, my sister here took Renegade to a whole other level. They won the Top Dog Award at the National Police Dog Trials in Arizona last year, and that's no easy feat." A proud grin spread across his lips as he remembered years ago when he'd helped his little sister train her new puppy—just for fun.

"No kidding?" Kendra's eyes widened. "You never said anything."

Caitlyn's cheeks pinkened, and she cast her gaze down at Renegade. "It was Logan's wedding day. It wasn't about us."

"Yeah, but still. That is an accomplishment of a lifetime. I'd be telling everyone who would listen."

"Thanks."

Logan's chest puffed with pride for his baby sister.

She'd come so far from the lost college student she'd been back then.

Clay moved to the front of the room and stood tall with his feet spread apart, giving him a solid foundation. He perched his hands on his hips just above his utility belt. With his close-cropped blond hair, he looked every bit the US Marine officer he used to be. "I've texted each of you your assignment locations. Be thorough and stay in communication with the team. I have a gut feeling that the explosion at the satellite parking lot was not an isolated event."

"What are you thinking, sir?" Logan agreed with Jennings but wondered what conclusions he had come to.

"The FBI is looking into the possibility that someone specifically targeted the family who was killed, but I'm not so sure. They flew home on an earlier flight than they had scheduled to take, so unless CBI determines there was a remote detonator, I think it might have been a practice bomb that inadvertently exploded at the same time the Morell's and the van driver arrived at their car. But if the bomb was on a timer, the explosion would provide information to the bombers, such as how quickly EMS and the bomb squad responded. Who was on call and where they came from. Those types of details. If I'm right, then we will either find more explosives or experience them. Let's make it the former. Keep your eyes open and be alert to your dogs' every reaction. Check every time they show more than a passing interest in something, even if they don't signal formally. We don't have the luxury of any quick passes."

Logan read his texted assignment. "Cait, you're with

me. Looks like we'll be starting out with three other satellite parking centers. They're all on lockdown until we release them." He glanced up at Clay. "This must be causing a colossal mess at the airport as far as parking goes."

Clay frowned and bobbed his head.

"Let's go." Caitlyn stroked her dog's face. "Ready, Ren?"

Renegade's eyes remained glued on her. He moved when she did and stopped when she stopped. The two were like one being, and it impressed Logan how far Caitlyn had gone with her dog's training. It was amazing how in sync they were as a pair—like they were dancing.

Jennings had assigned them to search the outlying parking areas west of the airport. It was a massive expanse of pavement with hundreds of vehicles to cover. With any luck, they would find nothing.

6

———

Logan dropped Caitlyn and Renegade off at the east end of the sprawling 4,500-space parking lot. He and Gunner would start searching on the opposite side, and they would meet somewhere in the middle.

"Okay, Ren. Let's get to work." She glanced up at the bright sun shining down from the cloudless, brilliant-blue Colorado sky and was glad for the cooler autumn temperatures. It would have been brutal to spend a hot summer day on the black tarmac baking under such an intense sun.

"*Such*, Ren. *Such!*" Caitlyn gave Renegade the Czech command that sounded like *sook* directing him to search for explosives. She kept Renegade's lead attached to the clip on his protective vest and followed him up the chain-link fence that lined the massive parking area. When they found nothing there, they searched car by car, beginning with a silver Hyundai at the end of the first row.

Airport officials had temporarily shut down all eleven

outlying parking lots until police K9s could inspect them —affecting approximately 40,000 public spaces. The FBI had tasked multiple K9 teams to search every parking lot on the property before they could release the parked cars and open the empty slots. Many vehicle owners would have to wait at the airport before they could get to their cars and go home, and who knew the number of travelers being forced to find alternate routes to the airport? Fortunately, there was a train that came in from Denver. Time was of the essence, but it was a massive job, and they couldn't rush too quickly at the risk of missing another deadly explosive.

Logan's voice crackled over Caitlyn's radio. "I'm in place. Meet you in the middle."

"Roger," Caitlyn responded. "See you there—if we don't find anything before then."

Renegade tugged on his leash, and she followed. He sniffed wheel-wells, tires, doors, hoods, and trunks. Caitlyn also made him pay particular attention to every lamppost and trash can they passed, since someone had fastened the original bomb to a light pole. Each section held 100 slots, and there were two sections in each row. Caitlyn sighed as she realized it would take Logan and her the better part of the day to get through the entire parking lot.

Sitting down, Renegade whined and barked at a blue sedan, causing Caitlyn's pulse to jump. He pawed at the right rear door. As she peered through a black-tinted window, Caitlyn radioed for the bomb squad. "We have a suspicious vehicle in the Alpine Satellite Parking Lot, Row 2C."

"On our way," came a disembodied voice.

The ATF Bomb Squad truck squealed as it rounded the corner into the lot and raced toward Caitlyn's location. She gave Renegade his reward toy to play with, and they backed away to give the ATF agents room to work. Everyone took cover inside and behind the armored vehicle as an agent clad in a reinforced bomb suit jumped to the ground from the back end. He trudged in his heavy suit to the car. Using a slim-Jim, he opened the car door and investigated inside. No warrant was necessary because the alert of a police dog is probable cause in a court of law.

The bomb agent searched the whole car, front, back, and trunk, but found only a dime bag of cocaine. Renegade had alerted to the drugs. Caitlyn let him have some time with his chewy anyway, since he had done his job even though they were specifically looking for explosives. He held his over-loved purple Kong Wubba toy in his mouth and tilted his head to the side as he stared at Caitlyn, making her laugh. "Who's a good boy? Ren! You're a good boy!"

While the ATF agents continued to clear her location, Logan called in with a suspicious vehicle on his side of the lot. Once the squad was certain there were no explosives in the car where Renegade alerted, they moved on to Logan.

Caitlyn and Renegade resumed their search, and before long, Logan's voice came over the radio again. "The ATF team discovered a handgun in the glove compartment over here. It wasn't properly locked up, so the driver of this car will get fined, but other than someone not following the gun laws Gunner's alert was a bust." On one hand, it discouraged her that the dogs had found no explosives yet, but on the other—more common-sense hand—she was relieved.

It was mid-afternoon when Caitlyn finally met Logan in the middle of the lot, and they declared the area ready to re-open to the public. They loaded their dogs into Logan's Explorer, making sure both had food and fresh water before they drove to their next assignment.

Caitlyn pressed against her stomach. "I've got to eat something before we start again, but I didn't pack any food."

Logan reached across her and opened the glove compartment. "There are some protein bars in here. Will that hold you over?"

"It's better than nothing. Thanks." She grabbed three and her brother smirked at her. "Shut up. This kid is a hungry bugger."

Logan rolled up to a brick building that housed the Administration of Parking Lot Attendees Office, which was located at the back of a restricted employee lot.

Caitlyn wolfed down the snack bars and guzzled the rest of her water bottle. "At least this place won't take long as long as the satellite parking did. You want the offices or the cars?"

"Gun and I will search inside."

"Sounds good, and when we're finished for the day, you can spring for the happy hour snacks."

"Deal." Logan chuckled and parked at the curb in front of the building. They released their dogs from the kennel, and her brother gave her a quick salute before he jogged to the double-door entrance to the offices.

"Come on, Ren. Let's see what we can find out here." She guided him through the small parking area where only 22 cars awaited inspection. They were about half-way through when Renegade doubled back on a scent. He barked and sat, whining. Excited, he barked again, pawing the air at the back end of the car.

"Good boy, Ren! You found something, didn't you?" Adrenaline coursed through Caitlyn's blood as she radioed the bomb squad once again. Renegade's body trembled as he focused on his find. "Hurry! I think my dog found explosive material this time, for sure!"

Logan finished with the small building and jogged out to Caitlyn's side as the FBI bomb truck rumbled into the lot. This time it was Addison who donned the bomb suit. She hurried toward them and the suspicious vehicle as fast as the heavy gear allowed. "You guys take cover behind The Beast while I locate what Renegade smelled."

Caitlyn raised her brows at Logan. He shrugged. "*The Beast* is her affectionate nickname for our armored vehicle."

Logan and Addison made eye contact, and he touched her shoulder before he and Caitlyn jogged to the back side of the heavy truck.

Agent Miller, the beast's computer tech, motioned for them to climb inside. "You guys can watch the video feed from Commander Reed's body camera mounted on her protective suit." Caitlyn followed her brother into the tight confines for a front row view.

Like her counterpart in the ATF, Addison opened the

locked car with a long, flat metal device, commonly known as the "Slim Jim", and began her search. Inch by inch, Addy combed through the compact car, searching and testing for explosive materials. She wiped strips of muslin coated with a florescent polymer on the door handles, the steering wheel and column, as well as the seats and dashboard. The special fabric was designed to detect explosive trace material.

Finding nothing concerning inside the car, she popped open the trunk. Bending into the storage compartment, she came up with a roll of blue-printed papers bound together with three rubber bands. In her other gloved hand, she held several ID badges hanging from identical bright-green DIA lanyards. Another Bomb Squad agent yanked on a pair of blue nitrile gloves and retrieved the items from her. He dashed back inside the FBI truck and ran the fabric pieces through a florescent light machine that could detect the most minute amount of explosive material.

"Bingo!" he shouted as he reached for an evidence bag and slid the fabric strips inside. "We'll get this to the lab and find out exactly what we have." He stuffed the roll of paper and the badges into separate bags.

Caitlyn pulled her phone from behind her Kevlar vest. "Let me get a picture of these employee badges and then let's find out why one car has three different IDs stuffed in the trunk."

Logan called headquarters with the license plate number and details of the car along with the names on the badges. When he finished his call, he turned to Caitlyn. "That was Cameron. He said they should know something soon."

After Addison cleared the vehicle, they had it towed to the Denver PD evidence lot for further investigation. Logan helped her climb out of her hot, heavy suit, and she grinned at Caitlyn. "Good find, Cait!"

"It was all Renegade." She bent to pet her dog. "Isn't that right, boy?"

Addison turned to Logan. "Nothing inside the building?"

"Not a trace."

"Well, we'll know more by the time we get back to HQ. Our shift is up, gang. Let's go debrief with Sanchez and then get something to eat. I'm starved."

"Me too, and it's Logan's treat." Caitlyn opened the back of her brother's Explorer and loaded the dogs into the air-conditioned kennel. "Let's get out of here."

"I'll meet you guys over there." Addison waved and disappeared inside The Beast.

Logan drove first to the K9 unit facility. "We can leave our dogs here. They'll get fed and can rest and play while we have dinner."

"Sounds good. Must be nice to have dog-sitting anytime you want."

Logan chuckled. "Yeah, but I don't use it much. I'd rather have Gun with me, you know?"

"I get it. Renegade is almost always with me unless I leave him with McKenzie out at the ranch."

"How are those guys doing these days? I have a hard time imagining Dylan as a girl-dad."

"He's a great dad! You wouldn't believe it if you saw it. Little Rose already has him wrapped so tightly around her pinkie, he can hardly breathe. McKenzie is going to have to be the disciplinarian in that family." A wistful emotion surged through Caitlyn's heart. Surprisingly, she missed being home, even though she'd only been gone a day and a half. How was she going to feel when she had to be away from her family once they had a little one of their own?

Caitlyn and Logan settled their dogs in at the unit before they drove to the FBI headquarters building and joined Agents Sanchez and Cameron in the briefing room.

"Great find, Reed. Er... Deputy Marshal Reed," Sanchez shook her hand.

"You can just call me Caitlyn. It's easier." She grinned at the FBI SAC.

Cameron spread some papers across the table a handful of agents stood around. "The car with the evidence you discovered was stolen. No surprise there. It's owned by a chef who lives in Golden. We're going deep, but so far, he checks out." Cameron shifted the papers. "The employee IDs all had traces of explosive material on them. They belong to various people who work at the airport. All of whom had previously reported their badges missing or stolen over the past week. We're looking into their backgrounds as well."

Caitlyn's shoulders drooped. "So basically, we still have nothing."

Sanchez rested his hip against the edge of the table. "Not necessarily. We're waiting to hear from the lab regarding the explosive material your dog sniffed out.

We'll be able to confirm whether it matches that from the bomb site and hopefully discover where the materials came from. The roll of papers Addison found in the trunk turned out to be a copy of the blueprints for the airport. This was a significant find, Caitlyn, and we now have a lot more than we had this morning." He checked his watch. "You guys get out of here. Get some rest and be back here tomorrow at oh-eight hundred."

7

"Sheriff's Office, this is Deputy Peroni speaking. How may I help you?" Izzy manned the phones from her desk across the room while Colt worked on his budget proposal for the next city council meeting. It was nice to have a second deputy on staff. It meant he and Wes could finally have scheduled days off. Now, if he could only convince the council to ante-up for a third deputy and at least one more Sheriff's Department vehicle, his office might begin to look and behave more officially. The insurance for the use of personal cars in their line of work was astronomical. Colt was sure it would be more cost effective for the town to make payments on a specifically designated Jeep or truck. Besides, the county could write it off.

"Sheriff?" Izzy covered the mouthpiece on the phone with her palm. "This is a Mrs. Sandlewood. She says she thinks her husband is missing somewhere up in the Black Hills."

Colt nodded to his deputy and lifted his phone

pushing the lit button so he could connect the call. "This is Sheriff Branson. You say your husband is missing?"

"I don't know for sure," the woman sounded hesitant, "but he hasn't contacted me at all, and that just isn't like him. He's very strict about these kinds of things. He's always telling our kids to let someone know where they're hiking and when they expect to be home so if they don't make it back for some reason people will know where to look for them."

"Wise words. I wish more folks would heed them. Was your husband camping, then? How long has he been gone?"

"He was hunting and expected to be away for one week. But you see, my husband—Paul Sandlewood is his name—is a seasoned outdoorsman and hunter."

"Even experienced hunters can get turned around in the hills."

"Yes, but Paul is also a retired park ranger and was in the Army, too. He's never gotten lost before."

There was a first time for everything, Colt thought wryly. "Do you know the general location where your husband planned to camp?"

"Yes. He gave me the exact GPS coordinates for his campsite, just in case. Will that help?"

Colt chuckled to himself. "Yes, ma'am, that's perfect." Most people were not so well prepared.

"Normally, I wouldn't worry," Mrs. Sandlewood continued in a harried voice. "But our daughter is getting married here in Colorado Springs next week, and he promised he would be home. He's supposed to walk her down the aisle. I'm worried because I haven't heard from him since he left. Maybe he's hurt and can't contact me for some reason."

Colt reassured her. "It sounds to me like your husband has the skills and know-how to take care of himself, but we'll run up there and look around—see if we can find him for you."

"I sure appreciate it, Sheriff, and I know my daughter does too."

"Not a problem, ma'am. Someone will call you back this afternoon." Colt set the receiver in its cradle on his desk. "Well, Izzy, are you up for a hike?"

"Sure, I guess. Where are we headed?"

Colt fed the exact coordinates into the map app on his phone. "Up to Black Hills National Forest to look for a possible missing hunter." He studied the map. "The GPS coordinates are for a spot just northeast of my in-laws' ranch. I know the land up there well. Let's go."

"Do I have time to make us some tea?"

Colt did a double take and rubbed the back of his neck. Izzy was a new and competent deputy, but she had some weird quirks. One of which was that she always carried a lime-green thermos filled with tea everywhere she went. "Make it quick, but none for me, thanks. I'll just reheat some of the leftover coffee from this morning."

"That stuff is going to kill you." A shudder ran through Izzy's compact five-foot-four-inch frame. "I don't know how you can stand it."

Colt grimaced when he sipped from his thermal mug filled with the thick, burnt brew while he drove them out toward the Reed Ranch. The mint-scented tea Izzy was drinking smelled a whole lot better, but he wasn't about to admit it. Half a mile prior to the eastern boundary of the Reeds' property, Colt turned onto a national forest access road almost hidden entirely from view by surrounding aspen trees and pines.

The rough two-track path was intended for four-wheel-drives only. Colt rolled down his window and poured the bitter liquid out of his cup before they bounced along the rugged terrain in search of the specific location Mrs. Sandlewood had given him. Tree branches scraped the sides of his vehicle from the edge of the over-grown road. Soon, the track became impassable even for Colt's 4WD, and he had to park the Jeep. He and Izzy hiked the rest of the way up.

Colt drew in a deep, refreshing breath of clean mountain air. "I used to run all over these hills when I was a boy playing with the Reed kids."

"Was your wife one of them?"

"Yeah. Caitlyn and her two brothers, Dylan and Logan. We were thick as thieves back then." Colt grinned at the memories of his wild and carefree childhood days that flitted through his mind. "Still are, I suppose. In fact, Caitlyn is down in Denver right now working with Logan and the FBI on the explosion that occurred at DIA a couple of days ago."

"It's cool they get to work together."

Colt shrugged. "I guess." He wasn't about to share his true thoughts and feelings on the matter with his deputy.

A little over two miles later, Colt and Izzy came upon a tidy campsite positioned at the exact coordinates Mrs. Sandlewood had given him. Rocks ringed a small fire pit in the center of a clearing approximately fifteen feet from a two-person tent. Someone had strung a nylon cord high off the ground between a couple of trees, from which a mesh dish-bag hung next to a canvas tote that likely held food items away from hungry predators.

Colt called, "Hello? Anyone in camp?" There was no response. He knelt by the fire ring and stretched his hand out over what remained of several burned logs. There was no heat—not even when he stirred the black and gray ashes with a stick. He strode to the tent and pulled back the door flap. Inside, a backpack filled with clothing and other survival essentials sat on top of a neatly spread-out sleeping bag. Next to that rested a CJ Box suspense novel and a propane lantern.

"Sandlewood obviously intends to return, but his fire hasn't been lit for at least 24 hours. Maybe he got hurt while out hunting and is stuck in the wilderness somewhere."

Izzy turned in a tight circle, looking overwhelmed by the towering mountains that surrounded her. "Where do we begin?"

"This camp is close to an old abandoned mine we used to explore as kids. There's a maze of tunnels to hide in. I wonder if maybe he took shelter there? No matter what, we're going to need some help up here. There's too much ground for the two of us to cover on foot." Pressing his lips together, he eyed his citified deputy and gave her a tight smile. "Can you ride a horse?"

8

Dylan Reed had long since finished his early morning ranch chores and was deep into fixing downed and broken fences on the property. Some of the old, barbed wire had been there since before he was born and had as much patching as original line. Mending fences was a never-ending job. He'd like to replace it completely, but that was an expense that would have to wait for a year when the cattle prices were much higher than they were now.

He had fitted the tail-hitch of his ATV with a barbed wire un-roller, which held a full spool of the sharp fencing, and the cargo box attached to the rear rack of the vehicle contained all the tools he needed for the task. In his grandpa's day, it would have taken at least two men and they would have had to carry their supplies in a buckboard wagon.

Larry, Dylan's Australian cow dog, trotted along beside him, keeping him company during the tedious work. Dylan didn't love patching fences, but he'd rather do that than be stuck in an office somewhere—any day of the week.

There was another hour's worth of work to do in the western pasture, and then he could go home for lunch and enjoy some playtime with Rose. Before he and McKenzie became parents, Dylan never could have imagined how much love he would feel for their child. His little girl had bound tight strings all around his heart, so much so that he ached to be with her as often as possible. Dylan smiled, thinking of Rose learning to ride one day and coming to work with him on the ranch. He made a mental note to start looking for a pony for her. If he started now, he'd have time to train the horse well enough for his daughter to ride safely by the time she was four.

Dylan's phone vibrated in its pouch hanging from his tool belt. He leaned the wire stretcher against the ATV tire and bit on the fingertip of his leather glove, pulling it off with his teeth. "Hello?"

"Hey, Dylan, it's Colt."

"What's up?"

"I'm up in the park, northeast of your place, you know, near that old mine with the tunnels? Where we used to play when we were kids?"

"Yeah. What're you doin' up there?" Dylan flipped open the top of his canteen and took a long pull of fresh, cold water.

"Izzy and I are up here looking for a missing hunter. We found his campsite, but no sign of him. He could be anywhere. I was hoping you might be able to bring up some horses and help us look for him. I've called Wes, and he's going to meet us here."

Dylan pushed back his sleeve and peered at his watch. "So, you need me, Sampson, and three other horses?"

"If you've got the time."

Another perk of Dylan's job was that he made his own schedule. "Sure. I can be up there in about an hour. Will that work?"

"Thanks, man. I knew I could count on you."

"No problem. See you soon." Dylan finished the wire patch he was working on and then piled his tools back into the compartment. "Come on, Larry. Let's go home."

He called McKenzie on his way to the barn, and by the time he got there, she had lunch packed for him and his dad was tacking the horses. The older rancher had two mounts ready to go and was buckling Whiskey's cinch tight enough to hold the saddle on, but loose enough for the gelding's comfort during transport in the horse trailer.

"I wouldn't mind coming along with you if you could use an extra hand," his dad said over his shoulder. "Your ma has me helping with house chores today, and I'd be more than happy to escape."

Dylan chuckled. "The more eyes, the better." He reached to take Rose from McKenzie's arms and nuzzled their baby's soft cheek and neck with his beard. Her delicious baby giggle made every day a delight. "We'll be back by suppertime." He breathed in Rose's baby scent before he returned her to his wife and he kissed them both goodbye.

His dad strode toward the barn to get his own horse. "Dylan, if you'll bring the trailer, I'll be ready to load 'em up when you get back."

Father and son hauled the horses several miles up a rarely used ranch road that led to a double-gated entry between their property and the national forest that bordered them. They unloaded the animals there. Mounting their own, Dylan and his dad ponied the other three horses to the coordinates Colt had texted to Dylan.

Colt and his new deputy stood as they approached. Dylan swung down from Sampson's back and shook hands with his brother-in-law. "Wes isn't here yet?"

"He'll be along any minute," Colt assured him. "Izzy should probably ride Whiskey. She's a little rusty."

Izzy's eyes rounded. "The term 'rusty' implies that I once knew how to ride and am now out of practice. My experience with horses amounts to the one time I went on a trail ride at Girl Scout Camp when I was eleven and I fell off when my pony bolted for the barn."

Dylan grinned and scratched his beard. "You'll be fine on this old boy. Hop up and I'll give you a few pointers." He boosted Izzy as she climbed into the saddle. She drew her knees up and leaned forward holding tight to the horn. "Take a deep breath and relax. Stretch your feet into the stirrups. Keeping your legs long and your heels down lowers your center of gravity and will help you stay on."

Izzy gave Dylan a crooked smile as she complied with his advice. "If you say so."

Colt perched his hands on his hips as he turned in a circle taking in their surroundings. "Being up here sure brings back some good childhood memories. Doesn't it, Dyl?"

"We're lucky we didn't get lost up here ourselves." Dylan showed Izzy how to hold the reins in her left hand. "Dad, you probably would have tanned our hides if you had known how much time we spent up here instead of doing our chores."

"Oh, I knew." His dad's laugh rasped through his throat. "Seemed like a good way to keep you monkeys out from underfoot."

Colt peered at the older man with a steely hazel gaze. "You knew? Somehow, that takes some of the shine off. We thought we were so clever in finding this place. It was our secret hideout."

Dylan's dad shook his head and spat a bead of tobacco on the ground from the dip he snuck anytime he was away from his wife. Dylan understood. Once he and McKenzie got married, his chewing tobacco days came to an abrupt end as well.

His dad wiped his mouth with the back of his hand. "I grew up on this ranch too, don't forget. I was running all over these hills well before you boys were even a blip on my horizon. Same with my Pa before me."

Izzy practiced walking Whiskey around the camp. "Sounds like the three of you know exactly where you're going, then. Hopefully, we can pick up this guy's trail right away."

Huffing from the hike up, Wes appeared through the trees. "You never told me I'd have to hoof it in, Sheriff."

"I never said you wouldn't." Colt grinned and clapped the deputy on his shoulder. "Thanks for coming up." He passed the reins of Wes's mount to him. "So, the man we're looking for has plenty of wilderness experience. The fact that he has disappeared tells me it's likely he's been injured. Keep an eye out for any tracks, signs of broken branches, crushed undergrowth or even blood. Wes, you come with me. Izzy, you ride with John and Dylan. Let's find this guy."

Colt and Wes plodded due north. "Radio me if you find anything," Colt yelled over his shoulder to Dylan's group.

Dylan's dad swung himself into his saddle—still agile for an old guy—while he remained on the ground looking in the dirt for tracks. In a swath of sand that made a natural trail, he detected the edge of a boot print. Stepping around it, he called back to his team, "This way." With his reins in hand, he and Sampson followed the faint tracks through the woods along the path of the soft earth.

They'd gone about half a mile when Izzy hollered, "Look, over there!" She pointed to the right side of the trail at a length of tattered plaid fabric caught on a branch, blowing in the breeze.

Dylan let go of his reins, and Sampson stood still, dutifully ground-tying to the spot. Stepping through some rough gorse at the base of the shrub, Dylan made his way to the fluttering material.

He reached to grab hold, but before he could, Izzy shouted, "Don't touch it! It could be evidence!"

Dylan peered up at her. "Evidence? Of what?"

"Look! It's covered in blood."

"Yeah, but that just means the guy is bleeding. Not

that someone committed a crime. Cops..." he grumbled and rolled his eyes, "always looking for a boogeyman around every bush."

Izzy's dark brown brows crunched together, and she appeared uncertain. Dylan shrugged and moved on, leaving the fabric alone as requested.

John nudged his horse over to the shrub and peered at the fraying scrap. "This blood is dry. It's been here a while. We best find this man. He probably needs our help."

9

Colt led the way through the tall pines with Wes following close behind. "If I remember correctly, the old mine shaft we used to play in is up this direction."

"It's a nice day for a ride," Wes commented casually. "Probably one of the last warm days before the cold comes to stay for the winter. It sure is pretty up here. It's been too long since I took the time to come up and see the aspen in the fall."

"Yeah, same here. Winter's leaning in, too. Hopefully, we'll find Mr. Sandlewood soon and unscathed." Colt gave the golden aspen an appreciative gaze as they rode by the gently rustling leaves.

"I could see him wanting to hide up here from all his daughter's wedding preparations. When my sister got hitched, it was an all-out circus. My dad and I did our best to stay out of the way."

Colt chuckled. "I hope that's all it is." Seeing the mine ahead, he pointed. "There it is." They dismounted and tied their horses to a tree branch. Wes followed as Colt strode to the opening of the ancient mine framed in rock and old weathered beams of rotting wood that once supported the entrance.

They paused inside to let their eyes adjust to the darker interior of the main tunnel. The walls were hewn granite, and the floor was a fine, soft dirt. "Look, Sheriff!" Wes darted off to the left and squatted down.

Colt approached and peered over Wes's shoulder at a wad of something bunched against the base of the stone wall. "What is that?"

Wes unfolded his pocketknife and held up a corner of the material with the tip. "Looks like a torn up, blood-stained shirt, to me."

Colt pointed his flashlight at the rumpled clothing to get a better view. "That's not a good sign." A dog barked from somewhere deeper down one of the tunnel offshoots.

Wes closed his eyes, listening. "How many passage-ways are in here?"

"It starts out with these four—the main shaft and the three minor ones. But after you get inside of them, they branch off and create a sort of maze. We'll leave markers along the way, so we don't get lost." The bark sounded again. "Let's find that dog. He might lead us to Sandlewood."

Colt kept a stick of chalk in the pouch on his utility belt that held his nitrile gloves. He used it now to mark the walls of the tunnel he and Wes followed toward the barking. As they went, the air got colder and denser and Colt buttoned up his Carhartt jacket.

Following the sounds, they finally found a scruffy, medium-sized brown and white, scruffy haired mutt. He'd cut one of his paws and struggled to stand when they arrived, refusing to put weight on his injury.

"Easy, boy." Colt knelt before the dog and politely held his fingers out to be sniffed. "What happened to you, little fella?" As he got closer, Colt realized the dog's paw wasn't merely cut. It looked slightly mangled. He also had several abrasions on his muzzle and shoulder. His fur was matted with dried blood. "It looks like he's been in a fight with another animal. I wonder if that's what happened to our missing hunter. Could have been a coyote, a bobcat, or even a bear."

Dylan's voice reverberated down the tunnel from the cave opening, and Wes called out, "We're down here!"

Light bounced along the rough stone wall seconds before Dylan, Izzy, and John joined them. Izzy dropped to her knees next to Colt. "We found a blood-soaked patch of flannel caught on a bush. I think it matches the shirt at the front of the mineshaft. Do you think the dog dragged it in here?"

"Hard to say. But look at his leg." Colt held up the dog's bloody paw. "I think something attacked him, and considering the torn-up shirt, I'm a lot more concerned about Sandlewood." Colt stroked the dog's head and scratched the wiry hair on his back. The friendly mutt rewarded him with a grateful lick. "Hey, Dylan, help me get this pup out in the daylight so we can assess his injuries better."

"Sure but be careful. Hurt dogs sometimes bite."

Wes bent to help Izzy to her feet, but she pulled her arm away from him. "I got it."

Raising both hands in surrender, Wes stepped back. "Just trying to be helpful. Don't be so touchy."

She glared at him. "Let's check farther down this tunnel. Maybe the hunter kept going."

Colt gently lifted the injured dog in his arms. "Hey, you two, take the chalk with you and mark your progress. Be careful. I'll join you as soon as Dylan and I take care of this guy."

John went with the deputies, and Dylan helped Colt carry the dog outside. When they laid him on the sandy ground at the entrance to the mine, Colt saw that moving the dog had caused his wounds to bleed again.

"Stay here with him. I have a first-aid kit in my saddle-bag." Dylan jogged to Sampson and retrieved a leather pouch. Together, Colt and Dylan cleaned the pup's cuts and scrapes the best they could and secured some clean gauze around his paw with a sticky blue roll of vet-wrap. "If you can spare me, I'll take this fella down to McKenzie. She can get him fixed up better than this and then call Dr. Moore. I think this poor guy is going to need some stitches and an antibiotic."

"Good idea." Colt handed Dylan his car keys. "My Jeep is at the top of the forest access road, about two miles down."

"Great." Dylan chuffed and shook his head. "Well, I'd better get started then. I'll tie Sampson to the trailer. You can ride down with Dad and pick up your Jeep at the ranch."

"Sounds good. Thanks, Dyl."

As Dylan hiked off, Colt radioed dispatch. "Hey, Tammy. Will you contact Mrs. Sandlewood and ask her if her husband brought a dog up hunting with him?"

"Sure, Sheriff. Are you having any luck up there? Any good news I can share with the family?"

"Not yet." Colt didn't want them to know he'd found bloody clothing until he had more information. "I'll keep you posted." He ended the call and returned to the mine.

"Sheriff!" Izzy's voice bounced against the stone walls from deep within the cavern, and Colt's pulse bolted. He sprinted into the opening of the dark tunnel.

Rushing toward the light ahead, he found Wes, Izzy, and John hurrying out. They carried a satellite phone, a leather notebook, and a map with a blueprint page folded neatly inside. Cocking his head to the side, Colt studied the various items. "What's all this?"

Wes opened the journal. "The words in here are gibberish, but I don't think it's another language. It seems like random numbers and letters."

Colt peered at the worn pages. "It looks like a code of some kind. John?" Colt glanced at his father-in-law. "Can you make heads or tails out of this?"

John held the open pages to the light. "It makes no sense to me, but I bet Logan could figure it out. Or at least he could run it through the FBI system and decode it."

"Yeah, maybe." Colt gestured at the papers in Izzy's hand. "What is the map of?"

John took the map and unfolded it. "This first one is a topographical map of this mountain range. Look." He pointed a work-roughened finger with a jagged nail at a red X marking the mine where they now stood. He then moved the map to the back of the papers in his hand and revealed another, more detailed map of the mine and its tunnels. "What do you make of this, Colt?"

"Well, if these items belong to the man we're looking for, then he's not simply up here hunting deer. The question is where is he? With the blood-stained shirt and the injured dog, I'm worried we're looking at a wild animal attack. Could be a bear or a mountain lion. When we find him, provided he's still alive, we can ask him about all this stuff."

"It's a little late in the season for bears, I'm thinking." John scratched his chin. "Also, I'd bet the dog dragged the shirt into the mine with him. Could be a mountain lion attack, though. If so, Sandlewood may no longer be among the living."

The same thought had occurred to Colt, and once again, he wished Caitlyn and Renegade were home. It would be a cinch for Renegade to track the missing man.

10

Dylan rested the hurt dog on a red woven blanket in the back of Colt's Jeep. He eased the vehicle as gently as he could down the bumpy track to the highway and turned right toward the family ranch. When he pulled into the barnyard, McKenzie was walking up the road picking a few remaining wildflowers leftover from summer. She had Rose strapped to her chest with a long stretch of twisted fabric. His wife looked to him like a beautiful Native woman with her baby, and a powerful surge of protectiveness coursed through him.

McKenzie waved and approached the car. "What are you doing in Colt's Jeep? Is everything okay?"

Dylan climbed out and bent down to kiss his daughter's downy brow. "Everybody's fine, but we found a stray dog at the old mine with a cut-up foot and a few other injuries. I brought him home to see if you could help him."

McKenzie peered through the back window to view

her new patient. The scruffy dog returned her gaze and wagged his tail. "Let me see if your mom can watch Rose for a few minutes, and I'll meet you two in the kennel office."

Dylan carried the whimpering dog into McKenzie's workspace and laid him on the long, empty island in the middle of the room. His wife joined him and looked the dirty mutt over before gently unwrapping his bandage.

"Animal attack?" She said without looking away from the dog.

"I think so."

"I'll clean these cuts out a little better and then give Dr. Moore a call." McKenzie had a benevolent partner in the county veterinarian. She sent him patients, and he sent her rescue dogs who needed rehoming. Gently, McKenzie checked the wounded paw. "By the way, you got a phone call about an hour ago from the mayor."

"Oh yeah? What on earth did he want? A campaign contribution?"

"He invited us to join him for dinner tonight at the golf club."

"He did? I wonder what that's all about." Dylan poured heavy skepticism into his comment. "Did you tell him we were busy?"

"No." McKenzie scowled at him. "I don't know what he wants. But you've never taken me up to the club, and I've never had dinner with a mayor before. So, I told him we'd be there." She glanced up at him. "And I'm excited!"

Dylan chuckled. "I'm not sure how special it will be, Kenze. I've known Barry Ringleman since we were kids. Trust me, he's nothing to get excited about."

"Don't spoil my fun, Dyl." She bumped his hip with hers. "Why don't you go feed the horses while I finish up here?"

"Is my mom watching Rose tonight?"

"No, in fact, Mayor Ringleman invited all three of us. He said he was a family man himself and would love to meet our baby."

Dylan smirked. He didn't know what Ringleman was up to, but he'd bet his best calf that it had nothing to do with wanting to meet Rose.

AFTER DROPPING the stray dog off at the veterinarian's office, Dylan ushered a harried McKenzie and a fussy Rose into the dining room at the Golf Club Restaurant. They were fifteen minutes late for their six o'clock reservation. Mayor Ringleman stood as they entered and waved them over to the best seats in the place. Their white linen-covered table overlooked the first tee and had an excellent view of the course. Crystal, china, and silver gleamed in the glow of soft candlelight from a floral centerpiece. A man Dylan had never seen before rose to his feet from the table as well. He had a small build and an angular face that held dark unreadable and shifty eyes.

From their table they could see the small town of Moose Creek below, which glowed with warm lights in the early evening dusk. A few lingering tangerine sunbeams stretched up into the deepening lavender sky on the horizon.

"Welcome, Reed family!" Barry Ringleman, whose

round belly, round head, and Chicklet-shaped teeth made him resemble a snowman in a suit. "McKenzie, I'm so glad to meet you."

McKenzie, holding Rose, bent herself in an awkward sort of bow. "I'm so sorry we're late. Rose... well, she had some baby issues."

"Not at all, not at all. Don't you worry one bit." Ringleman pulled a chair out for McKenzie and then stretched his hand out to shake Dylan's.

"Dylan, I swear you look more like your daddy every time I see you."

"Barry." Dylan responded, keeping his greeting to a minimum. He was wary about the mayor's sudden interest in his family. Dylan helped McKenzie get situated in her chair and set the diaper bag on the the floor next to it, all before Ringleman could introduce them to his other guest.

"Dylan, McKenzie, I'd like to introduce you to Mason Dray." Barry indicated the other person at the table with a grand sweep of his hand. "Mason, here is thinking of investing in the growth of our little town."

Mason, pressing his tie to his chest, reached across the table to shake Dylan's hand. The newcomer's grip was reasonably firm. He then pressed McKenzie's fingers gently with his. "It's lovely to meet you both."

Rose chose that moment to let out an ear-splitting screech. McKenzie's cheeks flared a bright magenta. "Excuse me." She grabbed the baby bag and dashed from the table, disappearing inside the women's restroom.

The men chuckled like the whole thing was cute,

knowing that it wasn't, and that they had no better solution than the one McKenzie took. They ordered drinks and chatted about the weather and the price of cattle until McKenzie returned with the baby.

"Sorry, guys. I guess Rose wanted to be sure she got her dinner before we started eating ours."

"No problem at all." Barry rolled his gaze toward her. "Smart girl. I bet it's a challenge raising your little one so far away from the conveniences of town."

McKenzie's brows knit together. "No, not really. Especially with her grandparents right there to help."

A grin slid across Mason's face. "The whole family lives on your ranch all together? In-laws and all. Not much privacy, I suppose."

McKenzie glanced quizzically at Dylan. He shrugged, not knowing the direction of this strange conversation but certain it was heading somewhere highly specific. It was clear to him that Ringleman and Dray had an agenda.

They ordered, and while they waited for their food, Barry regaled them with tales of the difficulties of being a child in Moose Creek. "It's a good enough life, I suppose. But it could be so much better if the town had more modern amenities. More things for kids to do. More restaurants, more shopping. Don't you agree, Dylan? I know it wasn't always easy for *your* family growing up."

A slow burn ignited deep inside Dylan's chest. "I have to disagree with you there, Barry. I had an amazing childhood on the ranch. And I know Logan, Caitlyn, and Colt would agree. The modern amenities, as you call them, only serve to pull kids away from their families, as far as I'm concerned. We had plenty when we were kids. More isn't always better."

Mason blotted his mouth with his linen napkin and spread it across his lap. "What about the school system here? You must admit they could use some upgrading. Not to mention, if Moose Creek paid its teachers more, you would draw a higher caliber of educator."

Dylan didn't respond to that because it was true, but the statement also felt like a trap. He finished his bourbon and carefully set his glass next to his plate before piercing the mayor with a sharp look. "What's this all about, Barry? Why the impressive dinner?"

"Well, sir. Here's the thing. Mr. Dray has fallen in love with our precious Moose Creek, and he would like to develop it further. He has a vision of building neighborhoods north of town and to the west. Of course, he'd be developing the infrastructure necessary for such a project: an actual fire department, a larger sheriff's department—I know your brother-in-law would love that—schools, restaurants, a rec-center. We have preliminary drawings back at my office if you want to see them after dinner. Or you can stop in anytime to look them over."

Heat flared behind Dylan's sternum like a gas stove igniting. "So, what does this have to do with us? McKenzie and me, specifically?"

Barry chewed his lower lip and dropped his gaze to his plate. He shot a sideways glance at Dray before finally looking at Dylan, not quite in the eye, but somewhere around his right cheekbone. "I'm here to facilitate a proposal. Mason would like to discuss the purchase of your ranch. The property is ideal for his vision, and he is prepared to make it so financially worth it to you and everyone in your family, that none of you would never have to work again. Now, that sounds nice, doesn't it?"

Dylan tossed his napkin on top of his half-eaten steak. "Not interested."

Barry held his hands up as if to calm Dylan and hold him in his chair at the same time. "I told Mason you wouldn't ever leave the family homestead. And I admire that. I truly do. But what about selling off a smaller portion of the land? You could think of it as a Reed family legacy to Moose Creek—a gift to others who'd like to live in this beautiful area, too."

"I said, I'm not interested." Dylan stood and held his hand out to help McKenzie to her feet. She had just taken a bite and was still chewing. She hesitated only long enough to swallow and then slipped her hand into his. The awkward tension at the table spurred a gutsy cry from Rose and McKenzie bounced the baby against her shoulder. "Thank you for dinner, Barry. But you really should talk to the town council about all your plans before you start trying to buy up ranch land. I don't know anyone who will be happy to hear about your desire to make Moose Creek into another run-of-the-mill city."

"Dylan, please sit down. You haven't had dessert yet." Barry reached for his arm, but Dray leaned back in his chair, crossed his arms over his chest, and narrowed his eyes.

"Couldn't stomach any." Dylan glared down at the

mayor—at the man who was once a boy he grew up with. "I can't believe you'd sell out our hometown like this, Barry."

The mayor sighed. "Not everyone in this town had the same idyllic childhood you Reed kids had. Try to remember that."

11

——————

Logan and Addison took Caitlyn to an Irish pub, a popular FBI agent hangout near the headquarters building, for dinner. The restaurant resembled a typical local bar in Ireland with dark beams, sturdy furniture, and a rowdy crowd. The only thing missing was live folk music, but the recorded version worked to set the scene. It was obviously a favorite of agency types who, to Caitlyn, all looked the same—buttoned up and polished. She wondered if the other patrons knew how well protected they were while they blissfully ate their meals

The three commandeered a circular booth in a corner with a window looking out on Quebec Street. It was much quieter in the dining room away from happy hour in the bar. They ordered their first round of drinks while reading the menu. Caitlyn asked for water with lemon, and when the server left, she jabbed her brother in the ribs. "Since I'm not drinking these days, you can buy my dinner instead."

Logan tugged her ponytail. "Happy to."

Addison decided quickly what she wanted to eat and set the menu aside. "Renegade sure has an amazing nose. He detected only a trace of explosive residue in the trunk of that car, and his find led us to discover those airport blueprints. Analysts are scouring through them as we speak. Depending on what they learn, we might have to shut down major sections of DIA."

Incredulous, Caitlyn shook her head. "Denver is a major hub. Can you imagine what a travel nightmare that would cause?"

Logan sipped his beer and wiped his mouth with the back of his hand. "Not as much as it would if a bomb took out half the property, not to mention the potential loss of life."

"That's true, but the Denver Airport is huge. Thousands of flights go in and out of there daily. Where will we start?" Caitlyn straightened her flatware while she considered the immense job ahead of them.

The server returned to their table to take their dinner order. When he left, Addison answered. "We have almost fifty K9 units deployed, which is one of our greatest assets in this case. Not to mention hundreds of boots on the ground. It will be a massive effort around the clock, but I have confidence we can get it done. Teams are out there as we speak."

Logan leaned over and kissed his wife's cheek. "This search is going to consume us all for the time being. So, how about we change the subject for a little while and take a much-needed break?" His gaze shifted to Caitlyn.

"How's the family? What's going on with Colt these days?"

"Everybody's good. We're having a lot of fun with Rose in the mix. She runs the place now with her pudgy little fists." Caitlyn relaxed against the back of her cushioned seat and thought of her husband. "Colt is busy. They've been out in the woods the last couple of days trying to locate a missing hunter. Our biggest challenge is Jace. He's such a great kid but he's been a handful lately. Before I left, he announced that he wants to drop out of school and become a rancher."

Logan choked on a swallow of beer. "What? He's only eleven!"

Caitlyn smirked. "I know. But he has big dreams of becoming just like Uncle Dylan."

"God forbid!" Logan winked at her. "Does he know Dylan has a college degree?"

"I told him." Caitlyn stirred the lemon wedge around in her glass. "I'm not too worried about it. He's in a funk at school right now, I think. But we're definitely entering a new phase of parenting that I, for one, didn't see coming. And Jace's mom isn't any help. She tries to blame everything on Colt."

Addison rested her hand on Caitlyn's arm. "And how are *you* feeling? Is your pregnancy causing you any discomfort? Is it hard to be at work?"

"Not really. I'm through the morning sickness part, so that's good. I get tired earlier in the evenings, but otherwise, I feel pretty well. This will be my last mission before I'm stuck riding the desk, though." Caitlyn stifled a massive yawn and laughed at the irony of its timing. "See? I'm going to need to get to bed soon."

Caitlyn had ordered fish and chips, but when the food came, she could only pick at it. The fried cod was tasty, but the greasy smell turned her stomach. Her appetite was fickle these days, and sometimes she ate only because she needed the fuel. On other days she was rabidly hungry and could eat anything at all.

After dinner, they dropped Addison off at her car and then drove to the FBI K9 Facility to pick up Renegade and Gunner. Kennel assistants had fed and bathed the dogs, and the pups were playing with a tug-toy in the yard when Caitlyn and Logan arrived. Caitlyn held Ren's face in her hands and scratched him behind the ears, which were still damp. "Logan, you and Gunner are spoiled."

"We have a pretty good deal here, that's for sure."

They loaded their dogs into Logan's Explorer and drove into the city. As soon as they got to her brother's house, Caitlyn and Ren went straight to the guestroom. Logan had lent them a dog pad, which Caitlyn placed on the floor next to the bed for Renegade. Even though she never allowed her dog to sleep on her bed, he looked at her with his best puppy eyes and whined hopefully.

"No way, my friend. You have a nice bed of your own. Now, lie down and go to sleep." Caitlyn stroked his sleek head. She called Colt before she turned out the lights. "Hey. How was your day?"

"Long. We still haven't found the missing hunter." Colt told her about the bloody shirt, the injured dog, and the mysterious items Wes and Izzy had discovered in the tunnel. "I'm worried a bear or mountain lion might have attacked the guy, but I'm equally concerned about what he was doing with the maps of the old mineshaft along with that book of codes."

"Codes? What kind of codes?"

"They're in the notebook we found. None of it makes sense to me. I thought maybe Logan could help us decipher it."

"Send him a copy. He can probably get it to an analyst to look at, but he's just as busy as I am right now."

"I will. The whole thing is weird, though. Don't you think?"

"It's strange, for sure. Did you find any signs of a struggle? It seems to me that if an animal attacked the man, you'd be able to track him. Did you look for a blood trail?"

Colt's frustration echoed through his voice. "If you and Renegade were here, we would have already found him."

A fissure of anger erupted in her chest, and Caitlyn paused before responding. "That's not fair. I have a job to do here. I don't work for the Moose Creek Sheriff's Department."

"Yeah, but with all the K9 units involved with this thing in Denver, is it really necessary for *you* to be there? I could use you at home right now, and frankly so could Jace."

"Come on, Colt." Guilt and exhaustion pressed down on her and she closed her eyes. Her husband sighed, and she imagined him rubbing the back of his neck as was his habit when he was frustrated.

"I'm sorry, Catie. It's just a hard pill to swallow

knowing we'd have already tracked this guy down if you and Renegade were here. And I'm having to work late, which is hard on Jace, especially now."

"Maybe you should ask the city council for the funds to hire a K9 team." She resented the guilt Colt put on her regarding Jace. He was Colt and Allison's son. Where was Allison during all of this, anyway? A disturbing thought crept into her mind—*how were she and Colt going to handle sharing parenting responsibilities once their own little one was born?* She rubbed her eyes and scrunched down under the covers. The last thing she wanted was to argue with her husband when she was so sleepy. An enormous yawn took over her.

"Yeah, right. I was barely allowed to hire Izzy."

"What about tracking the man with Athena? McKenzie could take her out to search. I know Athena doesn't have the training that Ren has, but she's a great dog, too."

"I'll ask her in the morning. We'll probably have to bring in Search and Rescue, too."

"There you go, with SAR you'll have plenty of dogs." Caitlyn faded and then snapped awake with a start.

"Hopefully, the guy will survive his injuries until then."

"Colt, I'm sorry, but I have to let you go. I'm falling asleep on the phone. Can we talk tomorrow?"

AT 4:00AM, Caitlyn, Logan, and Addison's cell phones went off simultaneously. Disoriented, Caitlyn bolted upright in her bed. Renegade's cold nose bumped her bare arm, causing her to shiver. She rubbed the damp spot and reached for her phone. An ALERT message lit up the screen. There had been another explosion on the DIA property. This time it was at a remote building, miles from the terminal and thankfully, it had happened in the middle of the night so no one was hurt.

Shuffling sounds came from outside Caitlyn's bedroom door. She jumped up from the bed and ran to the hallway. Addison was already dressed in her standard black leggings and fleece jacket. She headed down the stairs and asked over her shoulder, "Did you get the text from HQ?"

Caitlyn held her phone up. "I just got a notification. Did they call you in?"

"Yep. Logan, too. You and Renegade can come if you want, but I think the request only went out to the Denver FBI Bomb Squad since the explosion already happened. The targeted building was on our list to check today. Thank heavens no one was there during the night."

"I'm coming. I'll meet you downstairs in half a sec." Caitlyn dashed into her room and threw on her US Marshals T-shirt, a pair of utility pants, and laced up her boots. She'd left all her protective gear in Logan's car, so she had nothing to carry.

The three of them, along with Renegade and Gunner, sped toward the bomb unit building for the team briefing. Caitlyn sat behind Addison in the hard plastic suspect's seat next to the dog kennel. "I can't help but wonder what the purpose of these explosions is. They both happened at night when people weren't around. The family who was killed coincidentally arrived at their car when the first bomb went off, but it's possible that the bomber didn't intend for that to happen."

"Why do it then?" Logan clicked on the red and blue lights attached to the top of his Explorer and behind the grill and blazed through a series of traffic lights.

"I don't know. Perhaps it's a message of some kind, or like Agent Miller said, it could be that the culprit is testing airport emergency response times."

Addison nodded. "I've been wondering about the same thing. The motive also could be to cause chaos and instill fear in the traveling public. Or worse. Maybe they're practicing for something bigger."

Logan squealed around a street corner. The dogs both laid down to avoid losing their balance and Caitlyn braced herself between the door and the kennel. "It might be a way to focus the news media and the public's attention on DIA and Denver."

Nodding, Addison tapped on her phone screen. It rang through the car's speakers. Clay's voice responded. "Jennings, here."

"Jennings. It's Reed. Did you get the bombing alert?"

"I did. My team is on the way in."

"Good. I'll keep Logan with me and the bomb squad, but let's have Caitlyn deploy with you guys. We can meet up at the site of the explosion."

"Roger that." The line went dead.

12

Dylan woke early. He was usually up at five o'clock, but he couldn't sleep. He'd been tossing and turning since three-thirty and didn't want his restlessness to wake McKenzie, so he got out of bed at four. She'd been up three times during the night with Rose. Dylan's first pre-dawn stop after he got dressed was the coffeemaker in the kitchen. He turned it on and went to the refrigerator to scrounge for something to eat before he went out to feed the horses. He'd come back inside for a real breakfast, later. There was nothing interesting in the fridge, but he remembered there were some huckleberry muffins in the breadbox.

By the time he spread a couple with butter and wolfed one down, his coffee was ready. He filled an insulated mug and took it, along with the second muffin, with him out into the dark early morning. Washing his last berry-flavored bite down with a swig of the hot brew, he slid open the barn door. The horses inside nickered at him, and he turned on the light.

Larry, who slept in the tack room, scampered over to him and licked the few remaining crumbs from his fingers.

"Good morning, everybody," Dylan greeted the animals before he tossed several leaves of hay into the horse's stalls and fed his dog. Sampson's eyes were wide, and he kept his ears perked forward. He stomped his hoof and held his head high, not lowering it to bother with his breakfast.

Was it his imagination? Or were all the horses acting skittish? He slid open Sampson's stall door and ran his hand along the warm length of his horse's strong neck. The gelding stamped his hoof again and his skin shuddered under Dylan's touch.

"What's got your dander up, boy? Did a bear come through the yard last night?" With that thought, Dylan found a flashlight in the tack room, grabbed the Winchester rifle he kept on a rack over the door, and went outside to check the kennels and nearby corrals. He found no evidence of bears or mountain lions—nothing that would make the horses nervous. Shrugging, he returned to the barn.

The sun brightened the sky enough to see by the time Sampson had finished his hay. Dylan brushed him out and tacked him up, readying him for a morning ride. He led his horse past the kennel rows on their way to the front pasture. A few of the dogs McKenzie was boarding barked at them, but since the ride was a daily pattern, their alert lacked commitment. Dylan guided Sampson through the pasture gate, and then he mounted. He guided his horse along the fence-line toward the distant bank of Moose Creek where it ran through the Reed property.

Black cows dotted the wheat-colored autumn grass like specters in the early morning mist, mooing gentle complaints at being disturbed. The sun warmed the eastern sky, making the bovine shapes easier to discern. Three cows lay near the water's edge. Unlike the other cattle, they did not stir as he rode toward them. When he got within thirty feet of the slumbering cows, a buzzing sound caused Dylan to stop. The cow's bodies festered under swarms of black flies. It took Dylan several seconds to register what he was seeing.

Three dead cows.

He shuddered and Sampson took two nervous steps backward. What had happened? Dylan urged his horse forward, swatting at the flies when they flew in his face. Did a predator attack? Was that why the horses were agitated this morning? He peered down from his saddle, realizing there had indeed been a predator—a human predator. Someone had slit the throats of his cows and left them there to bleed out. Who could do such a thing?

Dylan's throat ached in sympathy as he looked on his cows. Most people would probably think *What are three cows among hundreds?* But he cared about each of his animals. He knew their faces, their personalities, and the kind of calves they threw. Ranching wasn't just a business to him—it was a calling. He loved the ranch and all the animals in his care. Seeing the three lives before him wasted for no reason made him sick. And angry.

A niggling sensation at the back of Dylan's neck had him reaching for the rifle he carried in its scabbard strapped to his saddle. He stared into the surrounding forest wondering if the culprit was still there. If so, he was ready to face him. While he scoured the dark tree line, his business mind angrily calculated the loss that three breeding cows represented to the ranch. He estimated an easy deficit of fifty-grand extrapolated out, and the thought ignited more fire in his belly. Wondering if his insurance would cover the cost, Dylan took pictures from several angles with his phone before he finally returned to the ranch. As soon as he had cell coverage, he'd call Colt and report the crime.

Dylan was in a sour mood when he strode into the barn, and it surprised him to find his eleven-year-old nephew inside brushing his horse. It was 9:00am on a weekday. Why was Jace there? Dylan stuffed the anger he'd carried with him from the pasture and did his best to act like it was any other normal weekend morning. "Hey, Jace. I didn't expect you out here today. Is your dad here?"

"No, sir." Jace's tone told Dylan something was wrong.

"How did you get here?"

Jace shrugged and focused on grooming his horse.

Dylan considered the boy for several minutes, trying to decide the wisest tact to take. "You look ready to go to work."

"Yes, sir. That's why I'm here. I've decided to become a cattle rancher like you."

As honoring as that was, the kid was just... well... a kid. He should be in school. "Okay. So, why are you here brushing your horse this morning?"

"You taught me to always brush him out before riding."

"True—that's right. But we're not riding our horses today. Shouldn't you be in class?"

"This is my class. There's no better place to learn to be a cowboy than a ranch."

Dylan scratched his bearded chin. "Okay... if you're here to work, that's exactly what you're going to do. Start out by mucking all these stalls. Dump everything on the manure pile out back and then find me. I'll teach you how to tidy up the pile after that."

"Okay. I'm on it." His nephew smiled with excitement. Dylan knew Jace loved ranch work, but today he would not reward him for skipping school. Instead, the kid would learn the dirty, gritty side of the job. Once he saw Jace was set up for his assigned task, Dylan returned to the house.

"McKenzie?" he called as he entered the back door through the kitchen.

His wife poked her head out of the pantry. "We're in here." She had baby Rose strapped to her chest as she carried out four jars of tomatoes and placed them on the counter. Her brows dipped together as she met his eye. "What's wrong?"

"Guess who I found in the barn this morning." Dylan took an apple from the fruit bowl, and McKenzie shrugged, moving past him to pull the Dutch oven out of the cupboard.

"Who?"

"Jace."

She spun to face him. "What? Is Colt here, too? Do you think they'll want breakfast?"

"No—to both questions. Even if Jace wants breakfast, he's not getting any. He's ditching school so he can be a rancher." He framed the word with air-quotes.

Understanding smoothed the lines creasing his wife's forehead. "I see. Does Colt know he's here?"

"I doubt it. Would you mind calling to let him know? I'm headed back out to make this the hardest workday that kid has ever seen."

"Trying to scare him off ranching?"

"No, I'm trying to scare him off ditching school. Apparently, I'm his role model, so he needs to understand that I use my agriculture degree every day."

"He just thinks you grew up out here and so you know all the things."

"I guess, but there is a ton he'll have to learn. Chemistry, biology, general veterinary care, crop and pasture rotation, business and economics—I could go on and on about what a rancher needs to know to stay afloat these days."

"So, you're going to give him a glimpse of the things he doesn't know?"

"I hope to. But will you call Colt? Hopefully, we can get ahold of him before the school does."

"No problem." She reached up on her toes and kissed his cheek, and he bent to plant one on his daughter's head. "Then, after I feed Rose, she and I are going to take a nap. She was up fussing all night."

Dylan decided not to worry McKenzie about the dead cattle. He'd discuss it with Colt when he came out to get

Jace. Dylan returned to the barn to micromanage, as painfully as possible, Jace's efforts, making certain that he'd cleaned up every single horse apple. After Jace dumped all the wheelbarrow loads onto the manure pile, Dylan climbed into his tractor and scooped the entire pile into the manure spreader. "We'll hook this wagon up to the ATV, and you can haul it out to the west pasture and disburse this crap evenly across the field."

"Okay. Then what?"

"Get the job at hand done before you worry about the next one." Dylan fitted the spreader to an ATV and sent Jace on his way as an icy breeze swooped down from the snowcapped peaks in the high country. Jace shivered as the wind cut through his thin sweatshirt. Before Dylan's heart softened and forced him to relent, he turned his back and stalked to the barn. His nephew was about to learn another hard lesson. A rancher must have the right gear to work in the ever-changing elements, especially in the cold climate of northern Wyoming.

13

As soon as Jace had left for school that morning, Colt drove to the office. He had hated leaving the mountains yesterday evening without finding the missing man, but they couldn't do much more once it got dark. He'd send his deputies up again today, hopefully with McKenzie and Athena.

Izzy was already at the office when he arrived. The large room was tidy and smelled like cinnamon and cloves. Since the day he had hired Izzy, she made small, homey touches to the office and he had to admit, it made coming to work each day a little nicer. He noticed a pot brewing on the counter and breathed in deeply of the roasted aroma. "Morning, Iz. Thanks for making the coffee."

"Sure thing," she said from her desk. If you and Wes insist on drinking that sludge, I'm happy to start it for you." She grinned up at him over a steaming, gold-rimmed, china cup. "I've been trying to make sense out of the maps and the codes in that notebook we found."

"Any luck?"

"Not really."

Colt filled a mug with the fresh joe and bending over Izzy's shoulder, he peered at the papers on her desk. "I'm amazed at this map of the mine and tunnels. I thought I knew all the passages to be found up there, but clearly there are several more we never discovered."

Wes entered the office carrying a brown paper sack and whistling to himself. "Good morning!"

Colt's right eyebrow shot up. Izzy tilted her head and asked, "What's up with you?"

Grinning, Wes held the bag aloft. "I have cinnamon rolls, and it looks like we have a fresh pot of coffee. What's not to be happy about?"

Colt chuffed, "Yeah, I'm sure the goofy look on your face has nothing to do with *who* you bought the pastries from."

"No, but it definitely might have to do with who I dropped off at the café for her shift this morning." Wes's eyes sparkled.

Colt's second brow joined the one already nudging against his hairline. "I didn't know things had progressed so far with you and Stephanie."

Wes shrugged and set the pastries on the counter. "Everybody want one?"

Izzy raised her hand. "I do!" She stretched her hands out. "We were just looking over the things we found in the mine, yesterday." She accepted the roll Wes offered and turned back to study the items on her desk. "Sheriff," she said around a bite of pastry, "what's this black circle mark for?"

Colt resumed his position over her shoulder. "I think that might be the location of an old, abandoned hunting cabin, but I'd have to see it to be sure. Maybe that's where we'll find our missing man."

"That would be a relief." Izzy sank her teeth into another bite of the warm gooey bun, and Colt went to the counter to get one for himself.

"I wonder how Sandlewood—a hunter from Colorado—knew about the mine and that old cabin?" Wes indulged a huge mouthful of his roll and swallowed it with several gulps of coffee.

"Hard to say." Colt crossed the room to his desk. "But I'm more interested in the codebook. If we knew what it said, we'd probably solve all our mysteries. I emailed a copy to my brother-in-law in the FBI. Hopefully they can decipher it."

The office phone rang, and Izzy picked up. "Moose Creek County Sheriff's Office, this is Deputy Peroni, how may I help you?"

Colt smiled to himself behind his mug. Izzy brought a level of professionalism to the department that had been missing before. He usually answered the phone simply by stating his name. Colt peeled off a spiral of cinnamon-saturated deliciousness.

"Oh, sure. Just one sec." Izzy held the receiver in the air, pointing it at Colt. "It's your sister-in-law, McKenzie Reed."

A shiver of apprehension coursed through Colt. McKenzie never called him. Maybe something happened to the stray dog they'd found. He gripped the phone and pushed a button that transferred the call to his line. "McKenzie, it's Colt. Is everything okay?"

"Yes. Everyone is fine, but I thought you should know that Dylan has an extra ranch hand today."

Colt shifted in his seat. "Okay…"

McKenzie chuckled. "Cute kid. A little too young for full-time work, though. His name is Jace Lopez Branson."

"What?" She was making no sense to him.

"Yeah, your adorable son showed up here about fifteen minutes ago."

"How did he get there?"

"I'm not sure. I haven't talked to him yet. He's out in the yard with Dylan. I just thought you should know he's not in school."

"Can you put him on the phone?"

"Not anymore. He and Dylan just drove off on an ATV."

"Well, make him stay put when they get back. I'll be right out." Colt slammed down the receiver. "I'll be back. I have to drive out to the Reeds' Ranch."

Wes leaned his hip against Izzy's desk. "Everything okay with your family?"

"I think so, but it looks like I need to play truant officer with my own son." Colt grabbed his jacket and cowboy hat, jamming it on his head. "We'll return to the issue of the mine as soon as I get back." Colt strode out of the office. He wished he knew what was going on in Jace's head lately. Why was he being so difficult?

Colt was ten miles outside of town when his cell phone rang. Allison's name appeared on his screen. *Great.* "What's up?"

"The school just called me saying that Jace was absent, but they hadn't received a parental phone call. You do *know* you have to call the administration office if Jace is sick, don't you?" Her condescending tone went right to the end of his nerves.

"Yes, *Allison*. I know that. Jace isn't sick. He's playing hooky."

"What? He's only eleven. Do you know where he is?"

"Yes, he's out at the Reeds' place."

"Well, *of course* he is. For crying out loud, Colt. You need to discipline that boy when he's with you. You can't let him run all over the mountains when he's supposed to be in school. I don't believe this." Her disgust flowed through the speakers and filled his Jeep.

Colt sighed and, rolling his lips inward, he bit down on the words he wanted to say. It wasn't his fault after all. Allison continued her rant. When she finally settled down, Colt interjected, "I'm on my way out there now. I'll find out what's going on, and then I will properly discipline him."

"What are you planning to do?"

"I'll most likely ground him. But you'll have to maintain that boundary when he's with you on Saturday and Sunday."

"That's not fair! My parents and I are taking Jace down to Fort Collins this weekend. You can't expect me to change my plans because you can't keep track of our son."

Colt muted the sound for a few seconds so he could let out his frustration with a car-rattling growl. The woman drove him crazy, and not in a good way. When he calmed, he turned the microphone back on. "We should ground him for a full week - no friends, no tech, no TV. I think it's fine if you take him to Fort Collins, but no gamepad in the car."

"That's a long drive, Colt. What do you expect him to do during that time?"

He could no longer resist a sarcastic bite in his tone. "I don't know... maybe *talk* to him? Or he could do his homework or even read a book. Whatever. You want me to discipline him, but you won't back me up when I do."

"It feels like you're punishing me, too."

"This is called parenting, Allison." He ended the call before he said something he'd regret. If Caitlyn were here, this never would have happened. She always walked Jace to the bus and waited until he got on. Colt had been rushed for time that morning and assumed his son had gotten safely to school. Would Caitlyn ever settle down into being a mother? He took a deep, guilt-filled breath and let it out slowly. He knew it wasn't fair to blame Caitlyn. She wasn't even in Wyoming. But he was concerned about how things were going to be when they had a baby of their own. Colt shook his worry away. For now, he needed to figure out what to do with Jace after school today while he was still at work.

14

Jace was in the pasture when Colt drove into the barnyard. Dylan was leaning on the fence watching Jace work. He pushed away and met Colt at his car.

"I hear you have a surprise ranch hand out here today." Colt climbed out of his Jeep and pulled on his leather, sheepskin-lined jacket.

"Yep. He's out there spreading horseshit on the pasture wearing nothing but the sweatshirt he showed up in."

"Good." Colt shook his head with consternation. "I can't believe he ditched class. That thought never crossed my mind until high school."

"I think he wants to quit school altogether. His plan is to become a rancher starting today." Dylan chuckled. "I have to admit, I'm mighty proud that he's thinking about going into the family business."

"Yeah, but not at eleven. And not until after he graduates. I'm going to have to ground him when I get him home."

"Don't be too hard on him. I'm already making him pay for his decision. After he's done out there, he can stack hay in the barn."

"Did he say how he got out here?"

"I asked, but he never really answered."

Colt squinted to see his son on the far side of the west pasture. Jace looked small perched on top of the ATV. "The school called Allison, and so I got an earful all the way out here. She thinks I can't handle him."

"That's not true. It could have easily been her house he bolted from."

"I know, but she doesn't see it that way."

Dylan stared out at the pasture. "Listen, I needed to talk to you today, anyway. This morning, I found three of my cows dead down by the creek bed. They'd had their throats cut."

"Seriously? Who would do something like that?"

"Don't know, but I'd gladly return the favor if I find 'em."

"Did you see anything on your game cameras?"

"No, but the horses were antsy this morning when I went out to feed. I think they smelled the blood on the breeze."

"Let's drive down there and check it out. Did you move anything?"

"No. I took some pictures on my phone, that's all."

"Could be a message. Have you had a beef with anyone, lately?"

"Not really. It could be some kind of message, but the

meaning escapes me. Come on inside for some coffee. Jace will be another 45 minutes, at least." Dylan led the way into the kitchen and poured two mugs from the pot on the counter.

McKenzie unwrapped a plate of freshly baked apple-cinnamon muffins and offered them to Colt. "Hungry?"

"Thanks." He took one, ignoring his high sugary carb intake for the morning. "Hey, Kenzie. How's that stray pup doing?"

"He's a sweet dog and I think he's happy to have a safe place to eat and sleep. Dr. Moore checked him over and said he seems healthy enough. Just under weight."

"Will you keep him?"

McKenzie glanced at Dylan and grinned. "I promised to at least *try* to find his owner first. He's not chipped, so it may be difficult to do."

"Good luck. Listen, do you think you might have time to go up to the abandoned mine where we found him with Athena today? I'm hoping she can help find our missing hunter."

"I suppose I can ask Stella if she'll watch Rose, but our sweet baby has been awfully fussy today. I'll have to let you know."

Dylan reached for a muffin, too. "Did I tell you that the mayor invited McKenzie and me to the golf club for dinner last night?"

"Is that so? What did ol' Barry want?" Colt blew across the surface of his steaming coffee.

"He had some developer with him. They asked me to sell Reed Ranch."

"You've got to be kidding. Barry knows you'd never let the ranch go."

"That's what I thought, but he wasn't kidding. The guy offered a ridiculous amount of money, and when I turned him down, he asked if I'd sell even a small part of the land."

"Why? What is he planning to build?"

"Tract homes, I guess."

"No way. Who would want to move up here? What would they do for work?"

Dylan shrugged. "I'm not selling, so it doesn't matter. Rose has been teething and fussing up a storm—poor little mite. But last night, her crying gave us a convenient excuse to leave the restaurant."

"Good for her. It probably wasn't her teeth—just the company. She's not about to give up her legacy without a scream or two." Colt took a long sip, closing his eyes as he swallowed. "I hate to think we could lose our small town. I like Moose Creek the way it is."

"Me too, and more importantly, I like my ranch the way it is."

JACE RUBBED his freezing red hands together, chapped from the bitter wind. He wished he had worn a coat and a pair of gloves. It was a mistake he wouldn't have to learn twice. He pulled the hood of his sweatshirt up over his head and tightened the drawstrings around his face since he still had half of the pasture to cover. Maybe Aunt

McKenzie or Grandma Stella would make him soup and grilled cheese for lunch. The thought made his stomach gurgle in anticipation and he pressed on the ATV's gas with numb fingers.

He made a wide turn and headed back down another length of the pasture when he saw his dad's Jeep pulled into the barnyard. Forget lunch, he was going to get into big trouble when he went inside. Still, he'd rather face whatever punishment his dad gave him than listen to his mom's unending griping. With any luck, his dad wouldn't tell his mom that he ditched school. Jace let out a long sigh—there was no chance of that happening. And worse, his mom would use his skipping class as a weapon against his dad, and neither one of them would understand why he did it.

Jace cranked the wheel again and headed back up the next row before returning to his thoughts. Caitlyn was the only one who understood him, and she was never home. He wished he could live at his dad's and her house every day and just visit his mom on special occasions. Jace loved it when his dad, Caitlyn, and he were home at their cabin together, but he also knew on a gut level that he was a burden to them. He loved Caitlyn, but she had never expected him to show up in their lives. A cold knot tightened in his belly. Caitlyn probably resented him. What if she'd rather he didn't live with them at all? Maybe he was the reason she left for work all the time. Jace's chest ached when he thought of how things would be once their new baby was born.

Hot tears blurred his vision, and his nose ran. He

wiped his face on his sleeve and ground his teeth with resolution. He spoke aloud to himself. "If I can prove my worth on the ranch, maybe Uncle Dylan will let me live here, forever. I could sleep in the barn. I'd work hard and stay out of everyone's way."

15

Seconds after the bomb squad's tactical vehicle skidded to a stop near the flaming building, three FBI K9 units screeched to a halt behind them. Clay Jennings with his black Malinois was the first out. He and Ranger sprinted to the open back door of the beast. "Give me a sit-rep," he hollered into the busy interior.

Addison's gaze snapped onto him. "As soon as Fire gets the site under control, we'll investigate. We'll know more soon."

Caitlyn, with Renegade in step immediately behind her, pushed her way through the small bomb squad and jumped out of their truck. "I'm assigned to your team, Jennings."

"Come on then, Junior." Clay gestured for her to follow him as he jogged back to his car. "HQ tasked our unit to search the private hangars on the property. You and Ren can ride with me and Ranger." The two dogs sniffed each other but behaved professionally as they loaded into Clay's mobile kennel.

Caitlyn hopped into the front seat. Peering skeptically at Clay, she asked, "Junior? What's with the name?"

He grinned. "You know—Junior Reed."

She rolled her eyes. "Great." She chuffed with humor as Clay sped off toward the row of small independent hangars.

"These private flyboy barns offer refueling and maintenance to their wealthy customers. The buildings come with a climate-controlled space and can handle large private jets like the Gulfstream G650, Bombardier Global 6000, and Dassault Falcon 8X. These spaces are first on the list of concerns because they bring in a clientele that doesn't have to go through the same type of security as the flying public. Who knows what these folks bring into the state."

"I don't know anything about the planes you just mentioned."

"Suffice it to say, they represent huge dollar signs and an entitled clientele."

Several hangars were empty, their planes off somewhere else in the world, but many had various sleek aircraft parked inside. Each K9 vehicle took a separate hangar. Before he got out, Clay gripped Caitlyn's forearm. "I know that you know what you're doing, but be careful. I don't want you getting hurt on my watch."

Caitlyn indulged herself with an inner eye-roll. "Will do. But as you said, this isn't my first rodeo."

They released their dogs from the vehicle, and Caitlyn pointed to the closest building. "We'll take this one." Clay nodded, so she and Renegade jogged off toward the focus of their search.

The front hangar doors stood wide open, and the shelter was vacant of its aircraft. Caitlyn led Renegade around the outside perimeter first, before searching the interior. The building resembled an enormous garage with a small office, restroom, and sitting room built in the back. The large space was mostly empty except for some toolboxes on wheels shoved against the side walls and a blue Polaris Ranger attached to a maintenance wagon parked in front of the office. There were no other personal vehicles parked nearby, and Caitlyn wondered how the owners of the jet got out there. Surely, they hadn't arrived for their flight on the work-worn side-by-side. They probably had a car service or a limousine or some other perk that the crazy rich enjoyed.

She and Renegade methodically searched the southern interior wall of the building before checking the rooms in the rear. Renegade's tail wagged, and he tugged on the lead attached to his flak-jacket. Work always excited him. "Good dog, Ren. *Such!* Find it! Good boy!" she encouraged.

They ducked into the sitting room which was outfitted with a large television, comfortable looking chairs and a small kitchenette. Caitlyn guided Renegade through the kitchen area first, checking inside the small oven, dishwasher and mini fridge. Ren gave no alert. The rest of the room proved equally clean.

A quick pass through the small bathroom took less than five minutes. When they got to the office, Caitlyn gripped the doorknob, but it didn't turn. It was locked.

Not wanting to bust the door in, she radioed Clay. "Jennings, it's Reed. There's a locked room in this hangar. How do you want me to proceed?"

"Pry it open. Minor damage compared to an explosion. We can't take the risk."

"Got it." She looked around for something she could use to break the lock. A promising toolbox rested in the rear cart of the Polaris, so she looked there first. As they approached, she noticed a number painted on the side, 2AH4. It looked more like an official airport vehicle than a personal one. Renegade pulled her toward the wagon and whined. He stood on his hind legs with his front paws braced against the side of the cart and barked.

Caitlyn's blood ran cold at Renegade's alert as she peered into the wagon. All she saw were a few loose tools next to a shiny silver toolbox with raised diamond plating. With trembling fingers, she lifted the sturdy lid. Nothing but screwdrivers of all sizes filled the top drawer. She grabbed the largest one to pry the office door open with but couldn't resist checking the other drawers. The second held various-sized wrenches. The third compartment at the bottom had double doors. She pulled on them, but they stuck. So, she jammed the screwdriver in the slit between them and forced them open. Red digital numbers glowed from inside the dark box. The timer read 7.5 seconds!

"Renegade! *Kemne!*" Caitlyn dropped the screwdriver. It clattered to the floor. She screamed as she pivoted, digging her toes into the concrete floor, she sprinted toward the hangar doors. Her dog, who could easily outrun her, remained steadfastly at her side as they sped toward the entrance. Heat hit her calves and spread up her legs. It seared her back and shoulders before a forceful gust slammed into her, lifting her off her feet. The ear-shattering boom came a milli-second later. It drowned out her scream. "Renegade!"

Caitlyn's body flew through the early morning air. She had no control of her limbs. An eerie calm took over her mind. In that moment, she felt no fear. There was only clarity. Her brain gave her instructions. "Tuck your body into a ball. Pull your arms in and hold your knees. You are going to land on the tarmac. Protect your head." She landed hard. The skin on her elbow burned. She rolled up onto her right shoulder skidding and scraping her cheek on the pavement. She finally stopped on her back. The crash-landing hurt like hell. With a quick assessment she determined she hadn't broken bones. She lay perfectly still, blinking up at the starry sky for several breaths before pushing herself to her hands and knees. Dizzily, she searched in the darkness for her dog. "Renegade!" Her voice cracked with emotion.

She spun at movement on her right. But it wasn't her dog. Clay and Ranger raced toward her. She yelled at them, "Where is Renegade?"

Clay pointed, and Caitlyn turned just in time to catch Ren as he leapt at her. She lost her balance, and together they landed on the hard ground, knocking the breath out of her lungs. Renegade bathed her face with his tongue. "Okay, okay! I'm okay, you crazy dog!" Her lungs hurt as she laughed and pulled him into a tight hug.

Out of breath, Clay joined them, staring down at her. "You okay, Junior? Looks like you found a bomb." He ran his hands over her dog. "Renegade seems to be moving alright."

Caitlyn told him what she had seen before running to escape the explosion. "Good thing that office door was locked, or we'd have been inside when the bomb blew."

"The toolbox was in the side-by-side?"

"Yes, and the cart had a number on it." She tried to visualize the numerals in her mind, but her brain wouldn't cooperate. "I can't... It'll come to me."

A siren blared in the distance. "That's okay. An ambulance is on its way. You need to go to the emergency room and get checked out by a doctor. Renegade should see our unit vet, too. Explosions can do internal damage you can't see on the outside, especially to hearing."

Panic gripped her heart and stole her breath. "Let me go with Ren. I'm fine and can always stop by the ER later."

"Not on your life, Reed. I'll have Agent Dean accompany Renegade to our doc, and then she'll bring him to you as soon as he gets an all-clear. You're going in the ambulance. No argument."

"But—"

"I don't want to hear it. I outrank you, Deputy. And I'm giving you a direct order." Clay contacted Kendra Dean on the radio and told her what he needed.

Kendra's voice responded over the speaker. "Annie and I are on the way. ETA five minutes."

Clay then called headquarters and informed them of the situation. "And Burke, Reed says she remembers seeing a fleet number on the side of the Polaris. It sounds like it might be an airport vehicle rather than a personal one." He paused, listening. "Not yet, but her mind will clear in time. We need to find out who drove that cart to that hangar. Also, tell Sanchez I think we should call for an immediate evacuation of the entire airport and ground all planes. We can't take any more chances."

Caitlyn ran her hands over Ren's head, body, and legs to reassure herself he was okay. She turned her gaze west, to the ambulance racing toward them, followed by a Channel 9 News van, filled, she assumed, with vultures scrambling for a headline.

Kendra pulled up ahead of them and jumped out of her K9 Explorer. She ran to Caitlyn and knelt beside her. "Thank heaven, you guys look okay. You were so lucky."

"Yeah." The drain of adrenaline after the immediate rush left Caitlyn lightheaded and queasy.

"I'll take good care of Renegade, Reed. I promise. And I'll keep you informed every step of the way."

Caitlyn nodded, not daring to speak. Her body went into shock, and her emotions surfaced out of her control. Tears flooded her eyes, blurring the morning pinks and purples cast upon the Front Range by the sun rising in the east. She wrapped an arm around her belly. Other than the few scrapes and bruises she'd sustained, she thought she was okay, but what would going into shock mean for her baby?

16

When Colt saw Jace coming out through the pasture gate, he left the warmth of the kitchen and went to join his son at the barn, waiting while he motored up the dirt road. Colt gave Jace a steady, hard stare and waited for his son to look him in the eye. After a big show of putting the ATV in park and setting the hand brake, the boy finally raised his head. His fearful gaze met Colt's from under the brim of his brown felt cowboy hat.

Colt crossed his arms, raising his chin in challenge. "Imagine how surprised I was to learn you were up here at the ranch instead of at school where you're supposed to be."

Jace bit down on his lower lip, but his gaze didn't waver. Colt had to admire that, at least.

"How did you get all the way out here?"

Colt could see his son's mind working behind his eyes—light hazel orbs that matched his own—before he swallowed hard and answered. "I hitched a ride."

"From whom?"

Jace's eyes darted to the side and then dropped their focus to the ground. He shrugged.

"Answer me with words."

The boy's voice was low and difficult to hear. "A truck driver."

Fury blossomed so quickly in Colt's chest it took his breath away, and he paused to gain control of his emotions before he spoke. "Do you have any idea how dangerous that is? Kids go missing every day!"

Jace shrugged again. The insolent mannerisms were new, and Colt did not like them.

"Besides, what makes you think ditching school is the way to go about getting what you want?"

Jace tilted his head and peered up at him from the corner of his eye. "I dunno."

"No, sir. Don't go there. 'I don't know' is not an answer. Try again." Colt ground his teeth together, trying to control his frustration.

The boy shifted his gaze to the distance as he considered how to respond to Colt's question. "The thing is, Dad, I *did* get what I wanted." Jace glanced back to gauge his dad's reaction. Colt kept his expression as neutral as he could, though a tiny muscle twitched at the corner of his left eye. "I wanted to be here—outside, working the land like Uncle Dylan, and here I am."

"Sure, you got your way for a couple of hours, but now you're grounded—no friends, no phone, no tech. Get your stuff and get in the Jeep. I'm taking you back to school."

"But—"

"Don't talk back to me. Do as you're told."

Dylan, who had followed Colt outside and stood behind him, murmured in his ear, "Why don't you bring Jace out here again this weekend? I've got several back-breaking chores he can do. Maybe we'll change his mind about the comforts of school."

Colt scowled. He wasn't sure what the best course of action was. He was still relatively new to the dad thing, and this pre-teen behavior knocked him off balance. Colt would talk it over with Caitlyn later. She'd know what to do. "It's Allison's weekend, so probably not, but I'll let you know."

ONCE THEY WERE on the highway driving toward town, Colt turned to his son. "You want to be a rancher, but you don't want to put in the work necessary to get there. That's like stealing to get rich. You might have some cash for a short time, but inevitably you get caught, and then not only do you lose your fast money, but your freedom as well. Dylan grew up on that ranch, but he still finished high school and went to college to learn to be the best rancher he could be. There are no shortcuts, Jace. You get out of life what you put into it."

Jace remained silent, and Colt hoped he hadn't damaged their relationship with his anger. He had no idea how to parent an eleven-year-old. His own dad had died way before Colt was eleven. The only example he could look to for being a father was John Reed. And he had been tough. Colt wanted Caitlyn's perspective on this whole thing. She seemed to have a keener insight into Jace than he did.

Colt parked in the circle drive in front of the school and walked with Jace to the office to sign him in. He stood by his son's side while Jace explained to Principal Nestor that he had ditched class and why. The principal thanked him for his honesty, gave him detention for five days. Then he and Colt walked Jace to his classroom.

After Jace was back where he was supposed to be, the two men shook hands. "Thanks, Dan. Sorry for this."

"I'm just glad Jace is safe. These things happen, but there must be consequences."

"I agree. On top of detention at school, he's grounded at home, too."

Colt returned to his office. Wes and Izzy were busy trying to get ChatGPT to solve the code, so Colt slid his hands into a pair of the tight blue nitrile gloves and spread the topographical map they'd found across his desk. "Let me look at that codebook for a sec." Izzy brought it to him.

"I know most of these tunnels, but this map depicts several more I know nothing about."

Fifteen miles northwest of the mine and higher in elevation by approximately 500 feet was another mark on the map in fluorescent orange, but there was no indication of what was there. He flipped through the pages of the coded journal looking for anything that might be coordinates, but nothing stood out. Colt turned on his computer and navigated to Google Earth. He entered the coordinates of the X according to the map. When he zoomed in, Colt saw a rugged, weather-beaten wooden structure that looked to him like a storage shed.

"Wes, have you ever seen this structure? The owner of this map marked the location, but I've never seen this before. Let me see the regular map." Wes brought the second map to him and spread it over the top of the first. "Look, the black circle on this map coordinates with the old hunting cabin I know about, but it isn't in the same location as the one marked in orange highlighter on the topographical."

Colt's deputy studied the computer screen and the maps over Colt's shoulder. "Nope. I've never seen it, but I can't say I've spent that much time in the mountains above Reed Ranch. I usually hunt in the Big Horns."

"Let's make a trek up to these cabins today. Maybe Sandlewood is hiding out from whatever attacked him in this second structure while we've been searching for him down below. If so, we can ask him what he finds so interesting about the mine and all these tunnels."

Izzy chimed in, "It'd be a relief to find him, that's for sure."

"Let's go. I have to be back at the school at five to pick up my delinquent son." Colt led the way out of the office.

Wes settled his hat on his head and followed. "Don't be too hard on him, Sheriff. Didn't you ever ditch school when you were a kid?"

"I did, but not until high school. Jace is only eleven."

They stopped at Reed Ranch to get horses and took the shortcut trail through their property up to the bordering National Forest. Colt hadn't ridden up this way since the Wendy Gessler murder case, when Caitlyn and

Renegade had found the woman's body and the sheriff at the time subsequently accused Dylan of the murder. He smiled to himself, remembering how determined Caitlyn had been to prove her brother's innocence. That was the case that brought Catie and him back together after their rocky history—back before he even knew anything about Jace's existence. Their lives sure had changed a lot over the past several years.

Wes opened the gate from atop his saddle, and Colt and Izzy urged their horses through. They rode in silence for another half an hour before they passed the mine. From there, they followed the path to the hunting cabin Colt was familiar with. The old building was practically collapsed; its roof had crumbled down on one corner.

"Last time I was up here, this place was still usable. It doesn't even look safe now." Colt checked his GPS. "Let's check out the other building." The three law enforcement officers continued their climb up to where the second structure was marked on the map.

As they gained elevation, the air grew thin and cold. The horses huffed at the effort bringing in less oxygen than they were used to. The golden aspen leaves rattled in the breeze and glowed against the bright blue sky. Forty-five minutes later, Wes pointed. "There it is."

A rough looking gray, one-room shack stood nestled in an aspen grove surrounded by tall pines. No smoke puffed from its chimney, and there were no vehicles or animals outside. The place was basically still intact but appeared to be abandoned. Colt dismounted and approached the door. He knocked. "Moose Creek County Sheriff. Is anyone in there?"

There was no response. Colt rapped again and then tried the door. It opened, scraping along the roughhewn floor as he pushed it. "Hello?"

There was no one inside, but a blue nylon backpack lay on a table with clothes spilling out of it. Several cans of food, a bag of chips, and half a six-pack of beer sat on a counter on the back wall. Colt checked the outer pockets of the pack looking for an ID but found none. "Someone is obviously staying here, but it's hard to say if it's the man we're searching for."

"No, but it's a solid guess." Wes held up a white hard hat with a headlamp attached to it. "Look what I found under the cot. This looks like something a guy roaming through dark tunnels could use."

17

Jace was supposed to be at his mom's house that weekend, but she had been invited to a getaway with her latest "man friend," so she dumped him off on his dad. His dad usually had the weekends off and was normally happy when he got an extra couple of days with Jace, but this weekend, he and his deputies were searching for a missing hunter up in the high country and he couldn't take any time off. On his dad's way to the sheriff's office, he drove Jace and Storm to Uncle Dylan's ranch. If that was being grounded Jace was all for it.

"Don't expect to have fun today. Your uncle is going to put you to work, and he's not going to be easy on you."

"I know." Jace turned his face to the window, hiding his grin. Storm, who rode in the backseat, poked his muzzle between Jace's headrest and the seat belt to lick his cheek. His dad might not have seen Jace's smile, but Storm knew how he felt. Jace understood the adults were trying to punish him for ditching school and were hoping to teach him a lesson by working him hard. But what they didn't get was that he loved every minute of being on the ranch—no matter how difficult the chores were.

They drove up the long winding drive to the Reeds' that was bordered by tall pine and aspen turned to gold behind a rustic split-rail fence. Jace's dad parked his Jeep at the bottom of the stairs leading to the front porch of the log ranch house. Uncle Dylan was already there waiting, sipping steaming coffee from his mug and glowering down at them. "Mornin', boys."

"Dylan." His dad climbed the steps and shook his uncle's hand. "You look like you've got something on your mind."

"I do. I've been thinking about those dead cows I found down by the creek. Their calves are bawling like crazy, wanting their mother's milk. I have them up near the barn to keep them safe, and they kept us all up most the night."

"Have you come up with any ideas about who might have killed them?"

"Damned if I know, but it seems like someone's trying to send me a message. It's too extreme to be a prank." Dylan gulped a hot sip from his cup and grimaced. "Jace, you head to the barn and get Rusty tacked up. I'll be down in a minute to help you load his saddle up with all the fencing materials you're gonna need."

A thrill coursed through Jace's entire body, from head to toe. "You're letting me ride today?"

Dylan's jaw shifted, and he narrowed his eyes. "Only because some of the fence line you'll be working on isn't accessible by the ATV."

"Jace," His dad's voice held an edge. "You work hard and keep your nose clean today. Got it?" He rested a rough hand on the back of Jace's neck and gave him a gentle squeeze.

"Yes, sir." As Jace and Storm took off toward the barn, his uncle invited his dad to go inside for a cup of coffee.

Rusty was happily munching on a pile of hay when Jace entered the wooden barn. The sound of the horses eating their breakfast was peaceful. Jace drew a deep breath in through his nose scented with horses, hay, and manure. He soaked it all in then gathered his grooming supplies, Rusty's saddle, and his bridle from the tack room. Jace brushed the red-roan coat that gave Rusty his name and cleaned his horse's hooves while he finished his meal.

By the time Jace tacked him up and was ready for the day, Dylan strode into the barn. "Let's get your tools attached to your saddle."

"How will I carry the barbed wire?"

"You won't need to. Today, you'll be riding the fence line and fixing any breaks you find." Dylan tied a fence stretcher onto the back of Rusty's saddle with concho straps. "You remember how to use this, right?"

"Yep." Jace reached for a set of multipurpose fence pliers and slid them into a saddlebag.

"There's an extra coil of wire inside the other pouch, just in case you need some for patching. On your way out, stop by the house. Grandma Stella has a canteen and lunch packed for you. Then I want you to ride out beyond the tree swing to the east property line and start at the corner post. Walk the entire perimeter. I expect this job to take you all day and most of tomorrow. Any questions?"

"No, sir. I've got this. Can Storm come with me?" Having his dog accompany him fit his image of a rancher.

"Not yet. He can hang out here with Larry. Rusty is still a little skittish around dogs. He needs more work." Dylan checked the tightness of the saddle's cinch. "Make sure you have a walkie-talkie with you. You won't have phone coverage out there."

"Okay."

"I want you back here at five o'clock, so plan accordingly. You and your dad are staying for supper tonight."

A smile sprang across Jace's lips before he could stop it. He loved having dinner at the ranch. Not only was his grandma the best cook in the whole world, but sitting at the long worn wooden table with his family made him feel like he belonged to something bigger than himself. There was a long line of Reeds that went back for over two hundred years, who had all worked this land. And though Jace was technically unrelated to the Reeds by blood, they always included him as if he were. "I won't be late for dinner! You can count on that."

"You'd better earn your appetite, little man. This isn't a play day."

"I know. I promise you'll be proud of me, Uncle Dylan."

"Alright then, get on outta here." Dylan did his best to look stern, but Jace detected a glimmer in his dark eyes, and he knew it pleased his uncle that the ranch meant so much to him. "Be careful."

Jace led his horse out of the barn and climbed into the saddle. His grandma waved at him from the back gate of the house, and he trotted toward her. "Morning, Grandma!"

"Good morning, Cowboy. I have lunch and some snacks packed for you. Let me put this in your saddle-bag." She tucked the food into the leather compartment on the side of his saddle before handing him a canteen filled with cold water. "I also made you an egg sandwich for breakfast. You can eat it before you head out." She handed him an English muffin with egg, cheese and bacon wrapped in waxed paper.

Jace had already eaten breakfast with his dad before they left home that morning, but he was always hungry these days. Caitlyn told him it was because he was growing. He hoped she was right. With any luck, he'd be as tall as his dad one day. "Thanks, Grandma!"

"Be careful out there, Jace. Keep your radio with you."

"I will. What's for dinner?"

Stella's blue eyes glittered with humor. "Brisket and mashed potatoes."

"Awesome! See you then." He turned Rusty toward the path that skirted the area and led out of the barnyard. He made his way past the tree swing and the cross that marked his Uncle Logan's Army dog, Lobo's, grave. Reining Rusty off the trail, they stepped into the surrounding woods on their way to the property's eastern fence line, where Dylan told him to begin.

Along the first twenty feet of barbed wire, Jace already found three breaks. Hopefully, this wasn't a sign of how the rest of his day would go. He dismounted and untied the fence stretcher from the leather straps on the saddle. At the first break in the barbed wire, he opened the tool and clamped one of the broken ends in its front grip. He did the same thing on the other end, attaching the wire to the back grip. He then ratcheted the lines together before mending the split with a smaller splice of wire, twisting the new piece tightly enough to hold.

Jace considered the work he'd done and smiled at the now functional fence. His chest puffed with pride as he got back in the saddle and rode on. Miles later, he found another break caused by a fallen tree limb. The log was too big for him to move on his own, so he tied it to his saddle horn and guided Rusty to pull the branch away before he could mend the wires.

The terrain steepened and became rougher as Jace and Rusty climbed the ridge, and Jace saw exactly why Dylan didn't want him to bring the ATV. When they arrived at the gate between the Reed property and the surrounding National Forrest land, Jace stopped for lunch.

He removed Rusty's bridle and used an extra halter and rope to tie his horse so Rusty could graze freely on the mountain grasses while Jace sat nearby warming himself on a sunny rock outcropping. He unwrapped a thick roast beef sandwich and took a gargantuan bite. His grandma had packed carrot sticks and potato chips, too. At the bottom of the sack, he spied two saucer-sized chocolate-chip cookies. If only he had a bottle of milk to go with them. Jace had sunk his teeth into a second mouthful of bread, meat, and cheese when he heard someone shout. It was a man's voice.

Jace set his lunch aside and climbed to the top of the rock formation to look for him. The man yelled again. Below Jace, to the north, was a man in khaki pants, bent at the waist, looking into something on a tripod. At first, Jace thought the guy was on the national forest side of the fence, but he was actually on the Reeds' side. Someone, maybe that man, had cut the fence cleanly through all three wires. The trespasser looked official, but he didn't think a Forest Ranger would cut through someone's property line.

With no cell service, Jace couldn't call Dylan, but he could take pictures, or even better—a video. As soon as he recorded the men's activities, he'd radio his uncle on his walkie-talkie. He crouched down on the rocks and pushed the button on his phone to record the man's movements, snapping still shots at the same time. Below, Rusty pawed impatiently at the ground under the tree where he was tied, letting Jace know he was getting bored. Uncle Dylan told Jace to let him stand tied for longer and longer periods until he learned to stand quietly. Now was as good a time as any for more training.

Jace attached the video and photos to a text and sent them to Dylan, but the message didn't go through. Laughing at himself for even trying, Jace raised his phone to take a few more pictures. Rusty added grunting to his irritation and tossed his head. He whinnied at Jace. The man in Jace's viewfinder stopped what he was doing and held completely still. He turned toward the horse's sounds and stared straight into the lens of Jace's phone camera.

"Hey! You!" The man took off running toward Jace, who jammed the phone into his jeans pocket and scrambled down the pile of rocks. He was well ahead of the man chasing after him, and Rusty was only twenty feet away. If he could get his horse untied and climb into the saddle fast enough, he would escape. Jace sprinted to his horse, but a second man he hadn't seen before stepped from around the backside of the rocks and blocked his way.

Huge hands gripped Jace's shoulders. He jerked against the burly man's hold but couldn't get loose. He kicked at his captor's shins. The man turned him around, and holding him against his massive chest, he lifted Jace off his feet. "Settle down, kid. What do you think you're doing taking pictures of us?"

Jace wriggled with all his might. "What are *you* doing on my uncle's property? You're trespassing!"

The man Jace had been previously watching came over the top of the rocks and made his way down the boulders toward them. "Get his phone, Jim!"

"I'll hold him while you get it. He's a handful." The powerful arms tightened around Jace's chest.

When the tall, skinny man finally got to them, he drew his hand back and slapped Jace hard across the face. The smack stung, and Jace's eyes watered. He cried, "You better let me go or you're gonna be in a lot of trouble. My dad is the sheriff of this county!"

The men laughed, making Jace feel withered and frightened inside. He gritted his teeth and renewed his fight until the tall man punched him in the belly. The beefy arms around his shoulders released, and Jace fell to the ground.

"I've got his cell." The muscular man yanked the device from Jace's back pocket. He dropped it to the dirt and stomping on it, crushed the screen with the heel of his boot.

"We need to get out of here but keep the phone." The taller man stalked over to Rusty, untied him, and then slapped the horse's butt. Rusty took off down the mountain, abandoning Jace to his fate.

"If I were you," the giant standing over him growled, "I would keep my mouth shut about anything you saw up here. Remember, we know where you live. Where your family lives. If you say a word about us, we'll know, and your family will pay the price." The man kicked Jace in the side. Sharp pain radiated through his body. Coughing, he curled into a ball. "Come on, Herm. Let's get outta here!"

The two men dashed around the rock formation and disappeared. Jace shivered and tried his best not to cry, but the tears came amid the pain and fear. After a time, when he could no longer hear his attackers, he pushed himself off the ground. Rusty was nowhere to be seen. It was getting cold outside, his jacket was tied to the saddle, his walkie-talkie was in a saddlebag, and it was a good ten miles back to the ranch. Jace told himself to stop being a baby and to quit crying. He limped over to where he had tied Rusty and picked up several items that had fallen from his saddle when his horse took off. *Dylan will kill me if I lose his tools.*

Jace wiped his face with his sleeve, and ignoring his persistent breath-catching sobs and the pain in his ribs, he set off for home watching for signs of his horse along the way. He kept an eye out for his attackers, too. More than anything, he did not want another beating.

18

The EMTs wheeled Caitlyn into the emergency room on a gurney with squeaky wheels. A team of three nurses met them at the doors and discussed her injuries. Since Caitlyn was able to breathe on her own and wasn't bleeding from anywhere other than some seeping from her minor abrasions, an ER nurse explained that she had to wait to be seen by the busy doctor on call. An orderly took her vitals and settled her in a curtained-off bed and told her the doctor would eventually be in to see her. Caitlyn estimated by the number of patients she passed by that her wait would be at least forty-five minutes to an hour.

Wrinkling her nose against the antiseptic smells in the room, she leaned back against a stiff plastic pillow on the narrow, inclined mattress and dug her phone out of her tactical vest. Navigating to her favorites, she pressed Colt's number and took a deep breath while it rang.

"Hey, beautiful." Colt's deep voice made her smile. "Tell me you're on your way home."

"Unfortunately, I can't do that."

"It was worth a try. How's it going? I heard on the morning news that there was another explosion at DIA."

"I'm doing fine. It's been good to see Logan and Addison."

"Your mission seems a lot more dangerous than we originally thought—don't you think? You said it was going to be more like a training exercise but it's the real deal, Catie. I don't like you putting yourself and our baby at such risk."

"I know. I'm sorry. The situation is definitely hot. I promise I'll be extra careful." She neglected to tell him that the early morning explosion he'd heard about had almost killed her. Her throat thickened, and she bit down guiltily on her lower lip, knowing that *particular* tidbit of information needed to wait until she got home and Colt could see for himself that she was fine. Even then, he was going to be furious. "In fact, I'll talk to SAC Sanchez when I see him this afternoon and ask him to assign me to some lower risk tasks." She pressed on without giving Colt an opportunity to comment. "The good news is they haven't found any other bombs, and they're planning to shut down the airport. That should keep everyone safe since the culprit will no longer have access to the property."

"Didn't you know they closed DIA an hour ago?"

"Sure. I wasn't sure of the exact timing." *Because I'm at the hospital.* Caitlyn hated being evasive with him.

"Even so, who's to say how many explosives the bomber planted before the shut down?"

"Right, but with the number of dogs they have

roaming the entire complex, I think it's a good sign they've found nothing else in the last couple of hours."

Colt was silent for a full minute before he released a deep sigh. "Can't you just come home? It sounds like they have more than enough K9 teams down there without you and Ren. Besides, there are no low-risk tasks that would need a dog like Renegade."

"Yeah, but they still need help. The problem is they have to interview every single airport employee. That's over 40,000 people. Even with the FBI, Homeland Security, the ATF, and the local cops all working together on that, it'll take forever."

"Have investigators uncovered any particular motive?" Thankfully, Colt switched to a more technical inquiry and Caitlyn released a pent-up breath.

"We can't be sure, but speculation is that the bombings might have something to do with a political summit scheduled in Denver for next week."

"Did they cancel it?"

"No..." Caitlyn was suddenly weary, and she closed her eyes. "The FBI warned them, but the politicians don't want to appear weak, so instead, they decided to move the meeting to an undisclosed location."

"So, you'll be helping with the interviews?"

Caitlyn hesitated. No way would the FBI waste a valuable K9 asset to do interviews that any admin could do, and she didn't want to outright lie to her husband. "Something like that. I'll keep you posted." That was mostly an honest answer. She hadn't even talked to Sanchez yet, so she didn't know for sure what work he'd assign her to. "How are things going at home? How's Jace?"

Colt made a groaning sound. "Not easy. Your brother talked me into dropping Jace off at the ranch today."

"I thought you grounded him."

"I did, but Dylan promised to work him within an inch of his life."

"Nothing like rewarding Jace for ditching by giving him exactly what he wants. I'm not sure that's teaching him anything."

"It has to be better than leaving him at home to watch some garbage on TV. And he'll be doing chores at our cabin all day tomorrow when I can be home with him."

"I suppose." Who was she to judge? She knew nothing at all about raising a pre-teen, and she wasn't there to help anyway, so she kept the rest of her opinions to herself.

"Allison has been making threats regarding custody again, and I don't want her to use my leaving Jace alone during the day as a point against me."

"She is so irritating." Caitlyn's shoulders tightened. "I don't know how you put up with her, Colt. Honestly, you know she would hate having full custody of Jace one hundred percent of the time. It would be too much work, not to mention it would cramp her dating style." She softened her tone. "Are you worried?"

"Not really. She's just being her usual pain in the ass."

"What else is going on? How's work?"

"We still haven't found the missing hunter. I'm getting concerned. I asked McKenzie if she could take Athena up the mountain to see if they could find his scent, but she's jammed up at home, so we'll see." He paused. "Oh, yeah —another thing. Some developer has been running around town with the mayor. He approached Dylan—took him and McKenzie to a fancy dinner at the golf club. Said he wants to buy Reed Ranch."

"You're kidding me! I bet Dylan sent him packing."

"You know Dylan."

"Uh-oh!" she chuffed. "Did my amped-up brother punch the guy in the nose?"

Colt laughed. "No, but I'm sure he told him where he could get off."

"Good for Dylan." A slender, harried doctor pulled open the curtain to Caitlyn's examination space and offered her a faint smile. He appeared over-taxed and undernourished. She covered her mouth and the phone speaker with her fingers to mute the ambient sounds. "Uh, I have to go back to work, Colt. I'll call you again later tonight. Love you!" She hurriedly ended the call.

The gaunt doctor consulted his iPad and then peered at her over the top of his metal-framed glasses. "Deputy Marshal Reed?"

"That's me." Caitlyn smiled encouragingly.

"I understand you experienced an explosive blast and that you're four months pregnant?"

19

———

Dropping Jace off at the ranch made Colt late to work, so he drove directly to Moose Creek without taking time to share in the tantalizing breakfast Stella was cooking. He'd only had time for a bowl of raisin bran before he and Jace left home and the salty scent of bacon frying in the Reeds' kitchen almost conquered his resolve.

Izzy was already at the office, brewing coffee when he arrived. The aroma of a rich dark roast drew him to the pot.

"Thanks, Iz, but you don't have to make my coffee, you know. I didn't hire you to be an office manager."

"I know, but you look like you could use it. Though... I can recommend a nice herbal tea for your fatigue that would help you feel better than that caffeine. Just saying..."

Colt chuffed. "No thanks. I need the full lead this morning." The office phone rang, and carrying a piping hot mug of brew, Colt strode to his desk to answer it.

"Moose Creek County Sherriff's Department, this is Sheriff Branson." He tried a page from Izzy's book of excellent phone manners.

"Branson, this is Cecil Colwell down here off County Road 261. I'm calling to report that one of my outbuildings burned to the ground last night."

"Hey, Cecil. I'm sorry to hear that. Was anyone hurt?"

"No, sir. We were out of town visiting the grandkids and just got home about a half hour ago. I pulled the RV around to the back of the house and found a smoldering pile of wood in the place where my workshop used to be."

"Well, it's good to know that no one suffered any injuries. Do you have any idea what started the fire?"

"Can't say I do."

"Did you lose any animals?"

"No. But I lost some tools and equipment. I don't know how the flames got started, but I promise you the shop didn't just spontaneously combust. What I want to know is what you're going to do about it."

"I agree, it sounds suspicious. I'll send a deputy out this morning to investigate. Don't touch anything until someone gets there." Colt glanced up as Izzy ended another phone call she had taken while he was on the line.

She finished writing some notes and then read them to him. "That was Colin Beyer calling to tell me that a vandal smashed the solar operated gate at the entrance to his property last night. I told him someone would come over to take a report."

"That's interesting, Beyer's place borders the Colwell ranch, where a building burned down last night." Something niggled at the edge of Colt's mind, and he tapped his pen rapidly against the desk as he tried to grasp it.

"What is it, Sheriff?"

"The Reed Ranch is just west of Colwell's place."

"Yeah?"

"The other morning, when I went to pick up my son, Dylan mentioned he'd found three dead cows out in his east pasture."

"Are you thinking these situations are all connected somehow?"

"I don't know, but it's too much to be a simple coincidence, don't you think?"

Izzy shrugged. "It is a lot. Especially since the affected ranches are all neighbors."

"And all three incidents happened over the brief span of a couple of days. When Wes gets in, you two go interview Colwell and Beyer. See if you can find anything suspicious. I'll talk to Dylan again when I go back to get Jace this afternoon."

Wes sauntered into the office, chewing on a sandwich wrapped in wax paper with the Moose Creek Café's logo printed all over it.

"I think you've been putting on weight since you started dating Stephanie," Colt teased.

Wes leaned back and patted his belly. "You're probably right. But I ain't complaining." A wide grin broke out across his face.

Chuckling, Colt shook his head before he grew serious. "Listen, I need you and Izzy to go talk to a couple of ranchers about some vandalism that happened on their properties. After that, I want you to make another trip up to the mine. If you guys don't find Sandlewood by 2:00pm, I'm calling in Search and Rescue."

Izzy pushed away from her desk and rolled in her chair to the coffee counter. She clicked on her electric teapot. "Mrs. Sandlewood said she isn't worried. She says her husband could survive for three weeks without fresh supplies. She just wants him home for the wedding."

"Did you ask Mrs. Sandlewood if she recognized the dog?"

"Yeah. She said they don't own one." Izzy poured boiling water through a strainer filled with loose tea leaves into her thermos. "Come on, Wes. You can finish your lunch on the way."

Colt remained in the office, skipping his noon meal so he could wade through the nagging paperwork piled up in his inbox. Hopefully, he would finish it early and have some extra time to spend with Jace before dinner. The pressure to be a better parent weighed heavily on him. Jace was struggling, and he needed his dad.

A little after three, Izzy burst back in through the office door out of breath. "Sheriff!"

Startled, Colt sloshed coffee on the papers covering his desk.

"Sorry, Chief." Izzy snatched a handful of paper napkins from the counter and rushed to blot the wet reports.

"It's fine, Izzy. And stop calling me Chief."

"Right. Sorry."

"What are you so excited about? Where's Wes? Did you guys find Sandlewood?"

"No, but you won't believe what we *did* find when we searched deeper inside the mine."

Colt raised his eyebrows, trying to be patient with her prelude.

She pulled out her phone to show him some photos. "Look! Bottles, rags, and gasoline. Together, these could make Molotov cocktails!"

"Yes, but—"

"I know you're going to say we're jumping to conclusions but look!" She scrolled through more images. "We also found timers, wires, and get this..." She enlarged a photo of ten gray soft-looking bricks. "C4!"

A cold flush sluiced down Colt's spine, causing a shiver to course through his body. "Are you sure?"

"Yes, sir. We knew you'd want to investigate yourself, but we had no phone coverage, so Wes stayed up there to guard the evidence while I came to get you."

"Let's go!" Colt left the mess on his desk, and grabbed his jacket and hat before they dashed out the door.

When they arrived at the mine, Colt followed Wes and Izzy inside. He'd brought several spotlights to help them see and to give better light for photos. Stacks of C4 sat against the granite wall of the tunnel next to a box filled with spools of various colors of wires. Another box held timers and electrical wire cutters. More boxes housed miscellaneous items he didn't recognize. "I'm going to call in the Wyoming Bureau of Investigations and the FBI. I don't know much about explosives, but they do. One thing I know is that they should be able to track where it came from. You two stay here. I'll go back down to where I have phone coverage by the highway."

Colt four-wheeled his way down the mountain where he made the necessary phone calls and then sent several images to Caitlyn and Logan in a text:

> Look what we found up in the old mine shaft above the ranch.

Logan responded:

> Like to get a closer look at all that. Many similarities to what we're finding at DIA.

> Caitlyn: Think there's a connection? Bit of a reach don't u think?

Colt's phone buzzed with a call coming through. "Dylan, what's up?"

"First, I need to say Jace is going to be okay."

A hot flash of panic exploded in Colt's chest, and he turned his Jeep toward the ranch. Peeling out, he asked, "What happened?"

"Well, I was trimming Whiskey's hooves when Rusty galloped into the barnyard without Jace. So, I jumped on Sampson and took off in the direction which Rusty had come. I found Jace on the trail coming down from the gate to the National Forest. He was roughed up quite a bit, so I patched him up best I could and rode him back home. Ma's nursing him right now."

"Did Rusty throw him or something?"

"No. How soon can you get here?"

"I'm already almost there. Tell Jace I'm on my way."

Colt's heart slammed against his chest as he skidded

to a stop in front of the Reeds' log home and bolted up the steps. He crashed through the door. "Jace?"

"In here!" Stella's voice called from the kitchen.

Colt ran through the saloon-style swinging doors between the dining room and the kitchen. "Jace!" His son looked up at him with a swollen, bloody lip and a shiner that was turning deeper purple by the second.

Stella cleaned and bandaged Jace's minor scrapes and cuts. "I don't think he has any broken ribs, but he's bruised up quite a bit. It wouldn't hurt to take him to the clinic."

"What happened, son?" Colt lifted his son's face in his hands and peered at his injuries.

"I saw some guys trespassing on Uncle Dylan's land, so I took some video. When they saw me, they chased me and wrecked my phone. I'm really sorry, Dad."

Colt grappled to make sense of what Jace was saying. "They beat you up? Did you say something to anger them?"

"No. I tried to be real quiet, but they saw me anyway. I'm sorry about my phone. I know I can't have another one since I didn't take care of the one you gave me." Jace's voice trembled with tears he fought to hide.

Colt embraced him, doing his best not to cause more pain. "I don't care about the phone, Jace. It wasn't your fault." He held his son by his shoulders and looked into his eyes. "Can you tell me what the men looked like? Had you seen them before? Did they say anything to you?"

Jace recounted his story again while Stella plied him with milk and fresh chocolate chip cookies.

Colt kissed the top of his head. "You did good, Jace." He turned to Dylan. "Can I talk to you in the living room?" The men went into the other room, and Colt lowered his voice. "Do you think this could have anything to do with the developer who is trying to buy up land around Moose Creek?"

"I don't know. What makes you say that?"

"I'm not sure. Just wondering out loud, I guess. Wes and Izzy found a bunch of explosive materials in the mine tunnels today. We're stretched pretty thin, even with the three of us. Could you and your dad go up and see if those bastards who attacked Jace left anything behind? I've got to take Jace to the clinic."

20

K endra met Caitlyn in the hospital waiting room with Renegade. "Good news. Ren showed no sign of hearing impairment and has no internal injuries. How about you? What did your doctor say?"

"Clean bill of health. The doctor slapped my wrist, but otherwise I'm okay." She laughed it off not admitting that he'd admonished her for taking such enormous risks with her pregnancy.

Kendra drove them to the FBI building, and they slid into a briefing that was already in session. Renegade lay at Caitlyn's feet under the conference table as she listened to the discussion over the explosion that morning. Self-consciously, Caitlyn pulled her sleeve down to cover the bandage taped over her scraped elbow. It was a minor injury, and both she and Renegade were lucky they came through their experience unscathed.

After her initial check up in the ER, the OB-GYN on call at the hospital had examined her thoroughly, including administering an ultrasound to check on the baby. The doctor had scolded Caitlyn for continuing to work in such a dangerous capacity, admonishing her to take time off and rest, filling Caitlyn with guilt. The baby was fine, but Caitlyn knew she had to make better choices. Colt had been right. Thankfully, her stubbornness hadn't caused any more damage than it had. She brushed her hand protectively across her abdomen.

Rick Sanchez's voice broke through her thoughts. "The evidence we have so far suggests several groups who could be at the root of these bombings. My concern is that these minor explosions are merely dry runs for a much larger event. We need to put a stop to this before it escalates."

Burke Cameron sent images from his iPad to the smart board on the wall. "Beyond Hamas, Hezbollah, and the other usual suspects, there's a local activist group we think has credibility. It's a radical anti-government faction who calls themselves *The Sovereign Earth Alliance*. This group has been on our watchlist for several years. We've intercepted comms from them discussing the disruption of interstate infrastructure. DIA would certainly qualify for that." He flashed to another photo of a man Caitlyn estimated to be in his mid-forties, clean-cut, intelligent looking. "This is Ted Marrin, the leader of the Alliance. Marrin's a Colorado native who grew up in Boulder. He's an environmental lawyer who got his undergrad at CU and went to law school at UC Berkeley. The man is articulate, idealistic, and media-savvy—often touted by the media as a modern-day Thoreau. He has a large podcast following where he expresses his deep disdain for both major political parties."

Sanchez pulled a chair around and sat. He rested his elbow on the table and propped his chin between his thumb and forefinger while he studied the smart board. "This is one of the groups claiming responsibility for the bombings?"

"Not directly, no. We're currently analyzing the transcripts of all Marrin's podcast episodes with its following of thousands to see if he's referred to, or has encouraged, any action like this from his audience."

Caitlyn leaned forward, bracing her elbows on her knees. She instantly regretted the move as pain from her scrapes shot up her arms. She sat up and drew her hands back to her lap. "What's the group's ideology?"

"Radical liberal separatism with environmentalist and anti-federal leanings." Burke clicked to the next photo of a mountain cabin that could have been a Ranger station. "This is Marrin's headquarters located in the San Juan region southwest of Westcliffe, Colorado. Analysts suspect his group of sabotaging several federal forestry sites, though that is still under investigation. They host some sort of off-grid retreats and are increasing their social media propaganda aimed at college-aged people." Burke went through several more photos depicting Marrin's online presence. "They are primarily environmentalists, but have shown increasing violent tendencies when they don't get what they want."

At the end of Burke's presentation, Sanchez stood and paced the length of the conference table. "Do they have ties to any of the usual foreign suspects?"

"Not as far as we can tell, but their behavior suggests escalation. If the bombings are their responsibility, it would fit in with what we've observed."

"Especially since the explosions have been relatively small." Kendra pushed herself away from her position leaning against the wall. "Even though the Morell family was killed in the first explosion at DIA, it appears that the bombers aren't intentionally targeting people."

Caitlyn agreed. "If this were a foreign terrorist organization, the bombs would have been bigger and taken as many lives as possible. This doesn't match their MO."

"Yet. This could escalate quickly." Sanchez rolled his lower lip between his teeth and stared at the screen for several long moments. "Burke, have our team maintain surveillance on this Sovereign Earth Alliance group and keep me posted. See if you can find a connection to them and the explosive material we have in evidence. Find out if any of their disciples work at DIA. It's obvious that the bombers either work at the airport or are connected to one or more airport employees. It could be someone on security, ground crew, or even restaurant or shop workers. There are around 40,000 employees at DIA, all with security badges."

Still stunned by the number, Caitlyn shook her head. "It's going to take months to interview that many people."

"And we don't have that kind of time!" Addison rushed into the room as Caitlyn spoke. "I have Jennings's most recent report. The dogs have been out around the clock, and so far, have discovered four more small bombs inside the airport itself."

Sanchez's phone alerted, and he read the incoming

message. "Cameron, override the senator and get that political summit cancelled! And I want those explosives traced to their origin." Burke bobbed his head and hurried from the room.

Caitlyn pulled the chair next to her out for Addison and asked those in the room, "Why would the bombers show their hand like this?"

"What do you mean?" Addison slid into the seat.

"The bombs they've planted are all relatively small and ultimately, we've had time to get the public out of harm's way. So, what is their actual target? What's their message?"

Sanchez rose from his chair and resumed his pacing. "We know one possible target is the political summit taking place in two days. Maybe the buildup is purely to draw attention."

Kendra rested her shoulders back against the wall. "Could be, but again, why would they show their cards and why target DIA? Why not just wait for the summit?"

"Publicity? Attention for their cause? Who knows?" Rick stopped and stared at the smart board, crossing his arms. "At least when everyone has evacuated the airport property, we can keep the public safe."

Addison glanced at Caitlyn but addressed Sanchez. "By the way sir, the security badges Renegade found in that car trunk didn't turn up anything useful. Agents have investigated the owners of the badges and so far, they've all come up clear."

"So, the IDs were stolen?" Caitlyn asked.

"Looks that way. They're still at the lab. We're hoping for prints or something."

"Okay, people, that's all for now." Sanchez reached for the stack of files he'd dumped on the table and prepared to leave the room. "We have work to do." His dark eyes turned to Caitlyn and Addison. "You two get back out to DIA with your teams. Find and defuse any remaining bombs. There is no time to lose!"

Caitlyn stood, and chewing on her lower lip, moved toward him. She spoke in a low voice. "Sir, I realize my personal issues aren't what you need to deal with right now." His obsidian gaze swung full force to her, and she cleared her throat. "And though I want to be here and help with the investigation, I have to ask for a less risky job assignment. Is there another way Renegade and I can assist your team that's less physically dangerous?"

Black eyebrows rose. "I thought the doctor gave you a clean bill of health, Reed. Are your injuries worse than reported?"

"No, sir. I'm fine, but..." Caitlyn hated to admit any form of weakness, but her vulnerability was more important than her pride. "You see... I'm pregnant and—"

"What? Why did I not know this?" The same black brows now crunched together. "You're going to stand down, Reed."

"Well, sir, that's why I was wondering if there is something else that Ren and I can do that isn't on the frontlines, so to speak? We want to stay and help."

21

Colt normally took Sundays off and had been looking forward to simply hanging out with his son all day, but when Wes called from the office to tell him they had a second missing person lost in the hills—a day hiker—Colt reconciled himself to another long workday away from Jace.

He and Jace had just finished a breakfast of blueberry pancakes with crispy bacon—a favorite of both of theirs —and were ready to tackle cleaning out the detached garage when the call came in. "Jace, it looks like I have to work today, after all. I'm really sorry. I wanted to spend the day with you, but another person is lost in the mountains, and I have to help find them."

His son's body deflated. "It's okay," Jace said in a tone that implied it was anything but. The bruises on his face and ribs were still dark purple, and Colt wished he could stay home and take care of him. Jace acted tough—as if his injuries didn't hurt much—but Colt knew better. But a hiker caught unprepared at this time of year could mean a miserable death if they weren't rescued.

Colt's chest tightened, and he released a sigh filled with regret. He pulled Jace in for a gentle hug mindful of his sore ribs. "I promise the next weekend I have off, you and I will do something fun. Just the two of us."

He dropped Jace off with Stella, who Colt knew would pamper and spoil the boy. "Make sure he takes it easy. He puts on a brave face, but I'm still concerned about his ribs." Colt bent to hug Jace, but his son turned away.

Stella walked Colt to the front door and assured him that she would take good care of Jace. Torn between staying with his son and saving a hiker, Colt kissed his mother-in-law's cheek. "I'll be back as soon as I can." With a heavy heart, Colt headed back to Moose Creek.

As he walked through the office door, Colt asked, "So, how long has the hiker been missing?"

Wes swung his boots off his desk and sat up in his chair. "Her name is Jessica Alcott—20 years old. She was supposed to return yesterday, mid-morning. Apparently, she'd gone up to the high country the day before to take some video of the area and to photograph the night sky."

"Alone?" The general lack of safety awareness displayed by people regarding the dangers of the mountains dismayed Colt. "Where is she from?"

"Jessica is a student at a film school in Cheyenne. Her roommate, who reported her missing, said Jessica came up here to video several old mines in the area, hoping to find a unique location for a documentary she's producing for her film class."

"Sure is a lot of sudden interest in that old mine. Are there any other sites she might have gone to?"

"Yes, her plan was to visit three locations. The mine we've been investigating was the third spot on her list, and she was supposed to return home yesterday."

"What kind of car was she driving?"

Wes referred to his notes. "Her roommate said it was a faded red Toyota Corolla"

"I saw a car like that parked under some trees by the national forest access road. Have there been any other reports of an abandoned car?"

"Not that I know of."

"Where is Jessica's family from? Have you contacted her parents?"

Wes shook his head. "I'm not sure, but I'm on it."

"Good. I'll call Search and Rescue. Then we can go back up there and try to find her with them." Colt didn't like to bother the search team if he didn't need to since they had to come all the way from Sheridan, but now with two people missing in the hills he didn't hesitate.

When the lawmen turned off the mountain highway on their way to the mine, they found the old model compact car parked under the shelter of a towering pine at the base of the two-track road in the same spot where Colt had seen it before. Its faded red paint had worn off in patches and the gray metal underneath showed through.

"There's no way that little Corolla could make it up the rough terrain," Wes stated. "This has to be Jessica Alcott's car."

"More than likely. Did you get a license plate number?"

Wes's cheeks reddened as he checked the notes on his phone and compared the number he copied to the plate on the car. "Yep. This is it."

Colt maneuvered his Jeep as far as it would go up the mountain before they got out to walk. After hiking the distance in, Colt and Wes approached the mine. The crime tape Wyoming Bureau of Investigations had stretched over the opening was torn in two and blew in the breeze. Wes gathered up the tangled strips of plastic. "Should I try to string this back up?"

"Don't bother. The investigators wouldn't have left the scene if they thought there was more to find."

"So much for 'leave no trace.'" Wes's sarcasm meshed with Colt's perspective.

John Reed was a stickler about taking care of the wilderness. He hadn't simply taught Colt and the Reed kids to leave no trace, but rather to leave the forest in better shape than they'd found it. "Right? It's hard to believe they just left the tape up here to rot."

Sunshine reflected off a piece of metal about twenty-five feet away and caught Colt's attention. He went to see what other trash had been left behind. When he approached the object, Colt realized it wasn't trash, and it was also much larger than he expected.

"Wes! Check this out. I think it's a drone." Colt gently pulled the device from the undergrowth where it had crashed landed. Half of its body and one of the wings were shattered. He held it up to the light and ran a finger over the curve of a perfectly round half-circle in the flight control section. On the other side of the circle was a mass of fiberglass in tangled splinters. "It looks like someone shot this baby out of the sky. By the size of the half-hole here, I'd guess a 9mm round took it down."

Wes joined Colt and peered at the ruined drone. "That wasn't here before. We searched all around this area."

Colt gently turned the mangled machine over. "These things have SIM cards, don't they?" He found the slot and ejected the recorded information. "When we get back to the office, maybe we can find out what the drone operator was filming." He dropped the small card into his shirt pocket. "Let's see if it looks like anyone has been messing around in the tunnels. Then, I want to know who was flying a drone up here... and why?" Colt led the way to the mine shaft opening.

He and Wes discovered that WBI had removed all the evidence. "I'm sure they took everything off to the lab for testing."

Wes aimed his flashlight into the dark distance of the tunnels. "Doesn't look like anyone has been here since."

"Let's check that hunting cabin one more time. The girl might be there. And we can see if Sandlewood ever returned for his clothes. Today, he's officially been missing for twenty-four hours past the day he told his wife he'd be home. He's been gone over a week total."

"You think he just lost track of the days?"

Colt shrugged. "It happened to me once when I was out hunting. It's easy to get distracted by the chase."

Together, they hiked the distance to the one-room

cabin. When they got there, they found a padlock had recently been attached to the outside of the door.

Wes tested the weight of the lock. "This is new. Who do you suppose put this here?"

Colt scanned the surrounding tree line. "Whoever the clothes inside belong to, I imagine."

Dropping the lock against the door, Wes let it make a loud bang. "Maybe Sandlewood realized someone had been snooping through his stuff."

They turned to walk away when a muffled sound came from inside the cabin. Wes froze in his tracks. "Did you hear that?"

Colt nodded and unclipped the safety strap on his holster. Resting his hand on the pistol grip, he moved back to the entrance. He listened for several seconds before knocking. "Hello? Is anyone in there?"

Muted but frantic cries responded.

"Are you hurt?"

The garbled sounds intensified, so Colt stepped back and kicked the door in. The lock tore away from the old wooden frame, and the door flew open, crashing against the wall behind it. Colt and Wes took cover each on one side of the doorway. Holding their guns at the ready, they peered inside. A hunched form, silhouetted by light streaming in through a single window, perched on the narrow cot.

"Moose Creek Sheriff's Department. We're coming in." Colt shouted into the dusty room. He stepped through the entrance first, followed immediately by Wes. Together, they visually cleared the small space of any threat. Colt rushed to the young woman huddled on the scrawny bed. Tear-filled blue eyes stared up at him with terror. Her mouth was taped shut, and her hands and ankles were bound with the same gray duct tape.

Gently, Colt eased the tape from her face, leaving red angry marks in its place. "Are you hurt?"

Wide-eyed, the woman shook her head. Wes cut the bindings from her wrists and legs, and she rubbed the sore spots.

"What's your name? Are you Jessica?"

"Yes," she whispered. She cleared her throat and in a slightly stronger voice, she said, "Jessica Alcott."

"Hi Jessica." Colt lowered himself to a knee. "We've been looking for you. You're safe now. I'm Sheriff Branson and this is Deputy Cooper. We're here to help you. Who did this to you?"

Hovering tears dripped over her lids making her dark eyelashes spikey. Her body trembled and she shook her head. "I don't know who they were. I was flying my drone when they grabbed me. And... I wasn't the only one. There was another man here for a while."

A cold knot fisted in Colt's gut. "Can you describe him? Did he talk to you?"

"No. I think he was hurt. He was huddled in the shadows. They carried him away about an hour after they locked me in here."

A heavy weight pressed down on Colt's shoulders. He looked Jessica over for injuries, and seeing nothing serious, he asked, "Can you walk?"

Jessica nodded. "I think so."

She stumbled over her first few steps and Colt assisted her to the door. She was gimpy but grew steadier as they went. "Wes, you stay here and wait for SAR. I'm going to take Jessica to the clinic."

"Will do."

"If the man Jessica saw is Paul Sandlewood, he's in trouble." Sliding his arm around Jessica's waist, Colt pulled her arm over his shoulders and helped her to walk the rugged distance back to his Jeep. On their way to the emergency clinic, he asked, "Can you tell me what happened to you up there?"

22

———

Logan and Gunner traveled on a low clearance utility cart designed to navigate the underground roads beneath DIA. They found their designated search section below the B concourse—the largest one at Denver International. The inner workings of the Denver airport system that were hidden from everyday travelers amazed him. An entire city existed underneath DIA that enabled the surface operations to run smoothly. Since Logan had moved to Denver, he'd heard many of the conspiracy theories surrounding DIA, of course, and now seeing the underground tunnels for himself, he could imagine how the rumors got started.

Supposedly, Denver's airport housed secret bunkers for the elite who could afford maximum protection if the world went crazy. Another theory was that the airport's isolated location made it the perfect place for a New World Order prison or a next-gen concentration camp. Some myths went as far as to say that the murals and artwork in the main terminal contained secret languages and codes depicting Nazism, death, or some twisted prophecy of the end of the world.

Then, of course, there was the giant blue horse statue that stood guard over the entrance of the airport. It glared down at travelers with blazing red eyes and was known to the locals as "Blucifer." Even Logan had to admit that it was creepy. The artist who designed the demon horse had been killed during the completion of the structure, and many believed the statue was cursed.

Logan shook off the imposing superstitions and focused on the job he was there to do. "Come on, Gunner. Let's look for bombs." The pair leapt from the low-riding vehicle and started down a dark roadway sparingly lit with white LED bulbs encased in metal mesh sconces attached to the cinderblock walls every fifteen feet. "*Such, Gunner. Such!*"

Together, Logan and his dog jogged down the empty underground road next to the integrated, automated baggage handling system built to shoot luggage from check-in to the various gates along the concourse and deliver incoming suitcases back to the baggage claim area. The distance the bags traveled was over half a mile, one way but since the airport was evacuated, the complex machinery sat eerily silent. Gunner sniffed the outer wall of the corridor first, then he walked more slowly along the conveyor belts of the system.

Gunner tugged on his leash, sending Logan an alert that he was on to something. Logan followed his dog's lead, shining his bright tactical flashlight into every dark nook and corner. Gunner stared up at a grouping of metal pipes banded together along the wall. He barked excitedly before sitting and whining, never taking his eyes off his find.

Logan sprinted to where his dog alerted and, sure enough, there were double bricks of C4 attached to wires and a timer clicking off the minutes until the explosion with red digital numerals. A cold sweat broke out all over Logan's skin, and his hands trembled. They had five minutes and 57 seconds. "Good boy, Gunner!" Logan's praising tone belied the shudder of fear that ran through him as he handed his dog his chew toy. That much C4 could destroy this entire section of the concourse.

He backed away and noted the alphanumeric designation of his location painted on the wall in the tunnel. The numbers coordinated with the gates overhead. He radioed his team. "Denver FBI Bomb Unit, this is Agent Reed. Do you copy?"

It seemed an eternity before the guys in the Beast responded. "We copy. Go ahead, Reed."

"Gunner located a hot explosive. The timer on the device currently reads five minutes and 42 seconds." Logan choked on the words and swallowed hard. He forced himself to focus on the job at hand.

"What is your location?"

"B concourse, underground at B42."

"On our way."

Logan concentrated on his breathing, doing his best to remain calm. He wasn't normally claustrophobic, but being stuck in a dark tunnel with a ticking time bomb caused him to feel many of the symptoms. He gripped his fingers and then shook them out to rid himself of the edgy sensation overtaking his body.

A minute later, the Beast's headlights gleamed in the distance, and his neck muscles softened a little. When the vehicle came to a stop, the back door opened. Addison greeted him with a reassuring smile. "Good work, agent."

"It was all Gunner."

"We'll send the robot to collect the bomb. You and Gun get inside the beast."

As Logan passed by his wife, he quietly squeezed her fingers, and her blue-green eyes sought his. Logan and Gunner found a place out of the way of the team, and Logan gnawed on his lower lip as he watched the screen displaying everything the robot saw when it deployed. "Does the new guy have a name yet?"

A small grin settled on Addison's lips. "Not yet. Maybe he'll earn one today." She leaned over the shoulder of the agent who controlled the robot's actions and stared at his computer screen. "Zoom in." Silence reigned inside the beast, and Logan caught himself holding his breath as the digital clock displayed two minutes, 33 seconds.

The robot's operator attempted to remove the explosive but quickly realized that it was held in place by a U-bolt that was welded to a triad of metal conduits. "We're going to have to cut those pipes."

Addison ordered a tech to find out what ran through them. He clicked frantically on his keyboard and glanced up at her. "Electric in two, and natural gas in the third."

"We don't have time to get those utilities shut off *and* cut the pipes. Can the robot access the wires?"

The operator attempted to reach the small wires tucked behind the C4 with the robot's hand-like pincer.

"The space is too tight. I can't get in!" Anxiety vibrated in his voice. "We're currently at one minute, forty-nine seconds."

Addison rested a calming hand on his shoulder. "That's plenty of time. Get the bomb suit ready. I'm going out."

Logan's gut tightened into a rock-hard fist as the timer ticked down. He wanted to stop Addy from going, but she was their only hope. He hated that Addison was the one on their team who took the greatest risks. But no one else had the skills she had. She was an extremely talented bomb technician, but what if the timer was off by a few seconds? What if the bomb blew before she was ready? He watched as she climbed into the heavy bomb-resistant suit and reached for her helmet. Before she pulled the thick, reinforced headgear on, she stared into his eyes.

"I'll see you in less than a minute and a half." Her hazel eyes bored into his with endless meaning.

He swallowed a spiky lump in his throat. "You've got this. No one better."

She nodded once and then clipped her helmet into place. The robot re-docked as Addison jumped down from the truck. She signaled for the team to seal the back door to protect those inside from a blast—just in case.

By the time she got to the device, the clock read 57 seconds. Logan took a position behind the tech agent and stared at the monitor. His heart slammed against his chest wall, and his hands balled into fists. Gunner pressed against his leg and licked his fingers in solidarity and comfort.

Logan ran his hand over his dog's head, but he never

took his eyes off Addison. "Come on, baby. You got this," he murmured.

Addison stared up at the bomb through her visor as the digits clicked down—43 seconds, 42, 41... She opened her toolkit and took out a set of long-nosed pliers and a wire cutter. How she could hang onto the tools with her thick gloves was beyond him. Logan held his breath. This would all be over in less than 30, 29, 28...

His wife clamped down on a gray wire with the pliers and moved the clippers toward the bomb, but she lost grip on the cutters, and they clattered to the floor. 22, 21, 20, 19... Awkward in the bulky suit, Addison bent down to retrieve the tool. Missed them. Tried again. Sweat broke out in beads along Logan's hairline and trickled down his temples and spine. He stared so hard his vision blurred.

Addison clamped down once again on the gray wire, pulling it out to give her access to the red, yellow, and green wires behind it. To Logan, they all looked the same, and he wished he knew which one was the right wire to cut. He prayed Addy did.

8, 7, 6... She fit the clippers over the yellow wire. Her voice echoed through the speakers. "Here goes nothing. I love you, Logan." 3, 2... snip.

23

Jessica's eyes filled with tears when Colt asked her for the second time what had taken place. He reached into the small red cooler he kept between the front seats of his Jeep and handed her a plastic bottle of cold water while he waited for her to collect herself. "I understand it's difficult, but I need to know everything that happened so we can catch the men who did this to you." She seemed to relax a little once they turned onto the paved highway.

"I came up here the day before yesterday because I'd heard stories about the old mine and wondered if it would make a good place to shoot a short film for my class. I go to school at the Film Connection in Cheyenne." Jessica glanced at Colt from the corner of her eye, and he nodded for her to continue. "Anyway, I drove up the mountain as far as I could, which wasn't far, and then hiked the rest of the way with my camera and my drone. I poked around most of the day looking for the best photo angles—you know. After that, I sent my drone up to video the area for future reference. It wasn't in the sky long before I heard a loud bang and my drone splintered in the sky. It fell to the ground, but before I could search for it, two men ran out of the trees toward me. They grabbed me and dragged me to the cabin where you found me."

"Did they say anything to you? Ask you why you were there, or anything?"

"No. It was terrifying. I don't know who they are or why they forced me into that cabin, but clearly, I wasn't the only one. That man—" Jessica's voice faltered. "He... the man... I hope he is still alive." A sob escaped her throat. "Do you think they killed him? Were they going to kill me?"

"I'm not sure what they had planned, but I think the man you saw might be a hunter we've been searching for. We thought perhaps a wild animal might have attacked him. Did you notice whether he had any serious injuries? Was he bleeding?"

"It was too dark to tell. He looked like he was in pain, and I wanted to help him, but I couldn't do anything with my hands and feet bound with tape." Tears flowed down her cheeks, and she wiped them away. "Who was that man? Why did they lock us in that cabin?"

"I'm not sure, Jessica. But I intend to find out."

Colt's phone rang, and the screen on his dashboard showed the incoming call was from Allison. He released a brief sigh and switched the call from the speakers to the privacy of his phone. "Sorry, but I have to take this," he said to Jessica before he answered the call. "Allison. Did you pick Jace up from the Reeds'?"

"Of course, I did. *I'm* the responsible parent, remember? He's in the car with me now." Her nastiness was the last thing Colt needed, and he didn't rise to the bait. "I emailed you a copy of the school's notification of Jace missing school last week."

"Thanks, but you shouldn't have bothered. They sent me that email, too." Colt had made certain the school sent him a copy of everything they sent to Allison.

"Well, I also wanted you to see my response. It's all on the record for the next time we talk with the custody judge. You and Caitlyn clearly neglect Jace when he's at your house. And the ranch draws him away from attending school. He's also become disrespectful to me at home, and I can only surmise that he's learned that from the two of you."

"Allison, don't drag Caitlyn into this. She wasn't even home." He rubbed the back of his neck and glanced at Jessica. It was unprofessional to take a personal call with a victim in his car, and he regretted answering, but he was worried something might have happened to Jace.

"Where is she *this* time?"

Her ugly tone gnawed on Colt's nerves, especially since her words poked a sore spot. "She has her own career, Allison. Something you might consider. Clearly the job at your parent's auto shop doesn't keep you busy enough." Colt pressed his lips together to keep himself from saying anything more. He was angry with himself for getting dragged in at all. "Listen, Allison, I have to go. I'm at work. Thanks for grabbing Jace. I'll pick him up after school on Thursday." He hung up before she could respond.

It concerned Colt that Jace was being disrespectful to

his mother. That wasn't like him, and it was not okay. Either way, Colt planned to contact his attorney. Just in case. Jessica watched him from the side of her eyes, but thankfully, she said nothing about his call.

Colt turned into the parking lot at the clinic and stopped outside the emergency room doors. "I'll help you get signed in, and then when you're finished with your exam, I'll come back to get you. I'd like to talk more about your experience on the mountain once Doctor Kennedy checks you over."

"Okay. Thank you, Sheriff." Jessica stepped out of his Jeep, and an intake nurse greeted her on the sidewalk.

"I've got her from here, Sheriff," the nurse assured him.

"Thanks. Call me when she's done here, will you?"

"We will."

Colt drove up Main Street past the Mercantile to his office across from the café. Once inside his office, he studied the evidence his deputies had found in the mine. The hand-drawn sketch of the tunnels was straightforward, as was the map of the area, but he couldn't figure out what the blueprint page was for. The plans vaguely resembled a motel or something. Was it a building the group planned on bombing? If he could decode the journal, it would probably tell him what was going on?

He dialed Caitlyn, but his call went to her voicemail. He listened to her message just to hear her voice and then called Logan. He didn't get through to him either. This time, Colt recorded a message. "Hey Logan, Colt here. My deputies discovered more explosive materials deep in the same mine where they found the coded journal. I'd like to talk to you about it. Call me as soon as you get a chance. Thanks."

The door to the office swung open, and Barry Ringleman strode in. "Sheriff, I'm glad you're here."

"Mr. Mayor. How can I help you?" Colt did not want to deal with Barry right then. He had important work to do. But the man was technically his boss, so Colt curbed his impatience.

"How are the missing person cases going?"

"We recovered the girl, and I have some good leads on the man."

"Good work!" Barry beamed but glanced pointedly over his shoulder, taking in the empty jail cell in the corner. "Where are they?"

"They were missing, Barry. Not under investigation. We found the girl, and she says she saw a man up there who I think was probably the hunter. But at this point, we have not located him."

Barry's face lost color. "You need to solve this case and move on. Missing people—or worse, dead bodies—are bad publicity for the future development of Moose Creek and our economic growth."

"No one has died and besides, I don't see how one has to do with the other."

The mayor's eyes squinted over a wily smile. "Developing our town to its full potential means money in the coffers, Colt. Think of it in terms of a nice raise for you, not to mention the money to hire more staff, and to obtain necessary updated equipment." He eased his girth into a chair in front of Colt's desk and braced his hands on the armrests. "Speaking about money, you ought to talk to that stubborn brother-in-law of yours. Mr. Dray, a developer friend of mine interested in investing in the future of Moose Creek, is prepared to make Dylan an excellent offer for just a small corner of the Reed property. Of course, that's if Dray doesn't get word about the dead cows on the Reeds' ranch. Dylan should move fast before my friend hears there might be something toxic on the Reed land and changes his mind."

Colt's gaze narrowed under furrowed brows. *How did Barry Ringleman know about Dylan's dead cows?*

24

Jace slumped in his seat and leaned his head against the cold glass. He glared out the car window, seeing nothing. His mom was yelling in the phone at his dad *again,* and Jace did his best to check out. He hated the part of the week when he had to stay at his mom's house. The family court judge had never asked him how *he* felt about where he lived. Everyone at the court said he was too young to make that decision. But all his mom did was complain about his dad and Caitlyn, as if *she* was so much better than they were. The times when they couldn't be home with him were because they had important jobs to do protecting people. It wasn't because they were out partying or trying to find a boyfriend.

In truth, it was his mom who was never home. She was either at some bar or on a date. She went out with random dudes most nights, leaving him to get his own dinner and to put himself to bed. Jace wondered what his dad would think about that, if he knew. Of course, he'd never say anything. He did his best to keep his mom and dad from fighting.

His mom finally stopped yelling once she was off the phone, but then she turned her anger on him. "You know what, Jace? You're grounded from going to the ranch for two months!"

"No! Mom! You can't do that! I didn't do anything wrong."

"I can, and I just did. And as I recall, you ditched school. So there. Besides, I can't even count the times you've gotten hurt while out at that place. This last time was the worst, and it wouldn't have happened if you weren't left out there on your own! I honestly don't think you should be allowed to roam around by yourself, anymore. All number of things could happen to you out there and no one would know."

"I had a walkie-talkie, but it was in my saddle bag when Rusty ran away. I should have hooked it to my belt. But I've already been punished for missing school. I had to go to detention to work it off and turn in my missing assignments. Plus, Dad grounded me from my friends and video games. Grounding me from the ranch for two more months isn't fair!"

"It's more than fair as far as I'm concerned." His mom squealed around the corner onto their street. "Your dad is just going to have to figure out what to do with you when he can't dump you off at the Reeds'."

Helpless rage filled Jace's body, and his neck and ears got hot. "Dad's at home a lot more that *you* are! And you can't control what I do when I'm at his house!"

She backhanded him across the mouth. "Don't you dare talk to me like that!"

Stunned, Jace covered the sting with his fingers. His breath came fast, and hot tears blurred his vision. "I *hate* you!"

The car skidded to a stop in their driveway, and his mom turned toward him. Her face was an angry red, and a blue vein pulsed at her temple. She spoke in a clipped and low tone. "You get to your room, young man. And you can stay in there until morning—without supper."

Jace slammed the car door and stomped into the house. He threw his backpack across his room and flung his door closed with all his might. A frame holding a picture of Storm fell off the wall. The glass cracked. He picked up the photo and propped it up on his desk.

I'd rather be locked in my room than have to eat dinner with Mom, anyway. Jace dove onto his bed. Gritting his teeth, he resolutely refused to cry. His mind raced over ways to change the situation he found himself in. He couldn't wait until he was eighteen. Then no one could tell him what to do.

When his breath finally calmed back to normal, Jace made a plan. He emptied school papers and a notebook out of his schoolbag and repacked it with jeans, some shirts, and because Uncle Dylan had taught him how important dry socks were, he threw in several pairs. Jace laced up his tennis shoes and zipped up his down winter coat.

Grabbing his backpack, he slid open the sash of his bedroom window and pulled the screen away. After tossing his pack through the opening, he climbed out and jumped to the ground five feet below. He was free.

His mom sat in the living room watching TV and scrolling on her phone, so he skirted the yard in the opposite direction and made his way two blocks over to Main Street. From there, he headed south until he was a good mile outside of town. Once he felt he had put enough distance between him and the people who would easily recognize him, Jace stuck his thumb out while he walked.

Dusk descended as Jace hiked along the shoulder of the road. Several cars and trucks zoomed by him. Some honked, but no one stopped. He unzipped his coat and gripped the straps of his pack, wishing he had thought to bring his water bottle. That would be first on his list when he got to his dad's house.

A blue car passed him, and then signaling, pulled to the shoulder. The driver leaned over, opened the passenger side, and the dome light came on. It was a woman. Jace ran toward the open door and peered in.

"Hey, you're Colt Branson's boy, aren't you?" The woman wore her long gray hair pulled into a ponytail at the side of her head. She had purple glasses and dangling bead earrings.

"Yeah..." Jace didn't know the lady, but she seemed friendly enough.

"I thought so. You look just like him, you know? I'm Erika. I own the flower shop in town."

Jace's shoulders relaxed. "Oh, yeah. Hi. I'm Jace."

"Where are you headed? Does your dad know you're out here? It's almost dark."

"I'm on my way home. I left my friend's house later than I was supposed to, and I forgot it gets dark so early."

"Well, get in. You shouldn't be walking on this road in the dark. You could get hit." She patted the passenger seat. "I'll run you home. I'm driving that way anyhow."

Jace tossed his pack on the floor and climbed in. "Thanks so much, Miss Erika."

"You're a nice boy."

The moon was out in full when the florist dropped Jace off at his dad and Caitlyn's cabin. It lit the yard almost like it was day. "Thanks again for the ride."

"You're welcome, honey. Get yourself inside now." She wiggled her fingers at him.

"I will." The lady seemed to wait for him to go into the cabin, but sheriffs don't leave their doors unlocked, and Jace didn't have a key. He hadn't planned on going inside the house. What he wanted was in the detached garage.

When Jace got to the door, he turned and waved. Lucky for him, Erika tapped on her horn and drove away. He waited for her to turn off their drive before he jogged to the garage. That door wasn't locked—heck, it didn't even close properly. He flipped on the light.

First, he let Storm out of his indoor kennel. "Hey, buddy!" His dog jumped in a circle, his whiplike tail smacking against Jace's legs. He sent Storm out to do his business and then fed him before he searched for his dad's camping gear.

The lightweight frame pack Jace needed hung on the wall above all the other supplies. He attached a one-man tent and the sub-zero sleeping bag to the frame and packed everything else he figured he'd need to survive on his own inside, including a bunch of dehydrated food and some dog kibble for Storm.

Jace purposely ignored thoughts of how long he'd be able to hide in the mountains with winter coming on. He wished he could get into the cabin where his dad kept the rifle he had been teaching Jace to hunt with. Plus, he'd rather have the hiking boots in his room than the tennis shoes he had on. But he'd have to do the best he could to keep his feet dry and rely on snares and a bow and arrows for hunting like he'd seen the survivalists use on reality TV.

The sky was black and sprinkled with bright stars in the clear cold night by the time Jace and Storm set out. On his way toward the woods, he heard sounds coming from the cabin. Storm stopped and cocked his head to the side. Jace stared hard into the dark, but he knew his dad wasn't home and didn't see anyone else. The house was dark. Deciding the noises were in his imagination, Jace and Storm hiked into the forest.

25

Kendra offered to give Caitlyn a ride to Logan's house where she had left her car. She could no longer ride to work with Logan now that Sanchez had reassigned her. He'd been quick to offer Caitlyn a job in a different location. It was a no-brainer job any rookie could do, but at least it was a dog-oriented mission and wouldn't pull another K9 agent off the more important work of searching for explosives.

Caitlyn checked her phone as she left the headquarters building with Renegade and Kendra. While she rode through the streets of downtown Denver, Caitlyn scrolled through her phone messages. She'd missed two calls and several texts from Colt and a fissure of alarm prickled at the back of her neck. She prayed everything was okay, but she would wait to return his messages until she and Renegade were alone in their own vehicle, and she had some privacy.

Kendra pulled up next to Caitlyn's USMS K9 Explorer parked at the curb in front of Logan's house. "Here you go. I'm really glad Rick moved your search location. Stay safe and take care of that little one you're carrying." Kendra's warm smile elicited one from Caitlyn in return.

"Thanks for the ride. Hope to see you again soon." Caitlyn hopped out of the car, and Kendra opened the hatch from a control on her dashboard. Renegade leapt to the ground and met Caitlyn at the back of their own vehicle. She waved as Kendra drove away.

"Ready to go to work, buddy?" Renegade wagged his tail and waited for her to open the kennel door.

Caitlyn entered Centennial Airport into her GPS, which guided her south on I-225. Rush-hour traffic was over, and she sailed down the highway as she called Colt. "Hey. Sorry I missed your calls. Is everything alright?"

"Yeah. For the most part. Mostly I was calling because I think the blueprint page we found up in the old mine might be for a section of DIA."

"You're kidding. What makes you think that?"

"I'm serious. I left a message with Logan, too. I realize you guys are in the thick of things, but I'm beginning to wonder if our cases are connected somehow."

"The backwoods of northeastern Wyoming are a long way away from Denver, Colt. Besides, SAC Sanchez thinks the organization behind the bombings at DIA is from the Sangre de Cristo Mountain area in Colorado." Caitlyn chewed on her lower lip. "What makes you think the blueprint is of DIA specifically?"

"Like I said, at first, I thought the plans were for some random three-story building. Maybe a hotel or something because there are so many outside doors, but then I realized there were rooms on the top floor, but no outside doors. On the middle floor, there were only a few rooms in a long wide hallway type interior with a ton of doors. It was the third, basement level, however, that had me the most confused until I remembered watching a documentary about how they built DIA. There were a bunch of conspiracy theories surrounding it."

"Yeah, none of which are true."

"Maybe, but isn't there an entire underground system beneath the airport, large enough for cars to drive around in?"

"Yes. In fact, that's where Logan and Gunner are working tonight. Send him a copy of what you have. He can check it out against the set of blueprints Renegade found in a car trunk yesterday."

"Interesting. Will do." Colt's voice softened. "By the way, how are you? I miss you."

Caitlyn smiled, missing him too. She wanted to share her full day with him, but she couldn't tell him about her close call earlier in the day without upsetting him. She was honest though when she said, "I'm fine. Tired. We were called in at four this morning. It's been a long day."

"You said Logan was working the underground at DIA. Aren't you with him?"

"No, Sanchez assigned me to a less risky location. I'm on my way there now. The senator is arriving undercover at a regional airport tonight. Renegade and I are going to perform a pre-landing sweep. But we won't find anything because no one knows he's landing there. How are things at home? How's Jace?"

"I'm glad to hear that you're not at DIA. Jace is okay, I think. But he's going through something lately. First, he skipped class, and today Allison complained that he's been disrespectful to her lately. I won't see him again until Thursday after school, but maybe he'll talk to me then. I don't know how to help him through this rough patch."

"I should be home by then. Maybe we can talk to him together?"

"I hope so. You're so good with him."

"So are you, Colt." A keen yearning for home bloomed in her heart. "Kids go through things. He'll be okay. He's got so many people around him who love him and who will support him."

"Thanks. In the meantime, I need to call my attorney. I want to stay a step ahead of Allison's ploys to get full custody."

"That's not going to happen. You have nothing to worry about."

"I hope not." Colt sounded tired.

"I'm sure of it." Caitlyn turned onto South Peoria Street and into the Centennial Airport complex. "I just got to the regional airport that Sanchez tasked me and Renegade to clear. I don't think anyone is out here besides Senator Hyatt's landing crew and us, but I'd better go."

"Okay. Please be vigilant."

"I will. I promise. Love you."

"Love you, too. Call me when you can."

Caitlyn drove around the airport terminal to the tarmac behind where the business jets and other small airplanes landed and parked. Senator Hyatt was due to arrive in one hour, and she and Renegade needed to clear the hangar slotted for his plane. Officials had planned the secret flight at the last minute, and it was highly unlikely she and Ren would find anything suspicious at the small regional airport, but clearing the space was necessary just in case.

Hyatt was a senator from Illinois and was the leading star of the upcoming political summit. He had originally planned for a huge reception in Denver that his staffers could then tout in the news outlets and on social media. Now, he was sneaking in under the cover of darkness. Why the politicians didn't move their meeting to another state, or cancel it altogether was beyond Caitlyn's understanding.

She parked next to the small hangar reserved for Hyatt under the alias of 'George Jetson' and let Renegade out. She saw no one else around, though there had to be a crew somewhere waiting to help bring the senator's jet in. Caitlyn clipped Renegade's long leash to his protective vest and asked him to sniff for explosives starting with the outside of the metal building. She jogged to keep up with him as he trotted along, sniffing contentedly.

They made their way to the massive door at the front of the hangar. Caitlyn pushed one of the huge sliders to the side far enough to enter the building and was surprised to see a jet already parked in its center. She double-checked Sanchez's instructions, wondering if she'd mis-read the landing time. But no, she was in the correct hangar, and Hyatt wasn't due for almost an hour. "Renegade, *knoze*." She ordered her dog to stick tight to her left leg as she approached the plane.

No lights were on inside the fuselage. There was no

one around, but the small hairs on Caitlyn's neck and arms pricked up. "*Such*, Ren," she whispered. Renegade, attuned to her emotions, stared up at her. She asked him again when he seemed reluctant to look away. "*Such*, buddy." Ren dropped his nose to the floor and investigated the aircraft's wheels.

Caitlyn followed her dog, and as they neared the rear of the plane, the surrounding air warmed. The engines had recently been running. Her shoulders relaxed, and Renegade bumped her hand with his muzzle and wagged his tail. The senator must have made good time on his cross-country flight, that's all. But it would have been nice to know he had already landed.

"Well, Ren. Let's finish checking the building and see if anyone is still around." They completed searching the outside of the jet and moved on to the interior walls, saving the offices at the back for last. The effort was basically pointless if the senator had already come and gone, but it was still her job to do.

Her guard was down when the door to the left of them swung open. "Hands where I can see them!"

Renegade barked furiously, equally stunned by the sudden appearance of two men shuffling together out of the side room. A silver-haired man in a suit and tie, with sweat dripping down his forehead, stared wide-eyed at Caitlyn. Behind him, with his arm wrapped tightly around his captive's neck, was another, taller, man wearing a black face mask.

Caitlyn murmured, "Ren, *sedni*." Renegade whined but sat next to her as she had asked, "Senator Hyatt?"

"Yes!" the man in the suit cried. "Please! Help me!"

"Shut up!" The masked man smashed his pistol grip into the senator's face. Blood spewed from Hyatt's nose and mouth. He cried out in pain. Wild eyes flashed from the holes in the balaclava. "Lady, if that dog moves... he's dead."

26

───────

The man with the gun edged toward the hangar doors. In that moment, there was no way Caitlyn could help the senator without someone getting shot. So, ignoring Renegade's anxious whining, she kept her hands in the air and stayed fixed in place, commanding her dog to do the same. "*Zustan*," her tone remained low and calm.

The kidnapper was obviously not a professional. If he were, he would have relieved her of her weapon and likely shot both her and Renegade. The fact that both their lives were intact, and she remained in possession of her Glock meant Hyatt still had a chance.

As soon as the gunman disappeared with the senator out massive double doors, Caitlyn called for backup. On her way to pursue Hyatt, she yanked a blue glove from the pouch on her belt and snapped in on her hand. She swiped her covered finger tips through the blood that had dripped onto the cement floor. Holding her hand for Renegade to smell, she whispered, "*Stopa*." Renegade lowered his muzzle to the ground to track the injured senator.

Local cops were the first to arrive in response to her call, along with a SWAT team that rolled to a stop behind their cruisers. Caitlyn took a few seconds from tracking the senator to speak with the sergeant in charge. She asked him to set up a perimeter around the flight-line and gave him a brief description of the gunman who had hold of Hyatt. "My dog and I are searching for them. Hyatt is an older white male wearing a blue suit and red tie. "We need to search building by building. They couldn't have gone far. It's only a matter of time until we find them."

Caitlyn and Renegade joined the SWAT team as they entered the hangar next door. Instead of opening the giant sliding doors, they filed in through a service door cut into the side of the building. Pivoting as they stepped through, the officers made certain the large interior space was clear before they proceeded. They communicated with each other using hand signals and precise, choreographed movements. Breaking apart once they entered the hangar, three men silently climbed the metal stairs to the second level while six others divided the rooms on the lower level.

Renegade sniffed the floor around the outer door, but finding nothing, he tugged Caitlyn outside. She followed him, trusting his instincts and desire to capture the man with the gun. She ran behind Ren toward the next hangar.

A black SUV pulled alongside her, slowing to her

pace. The passenger window rolled down. "Heard you needed back up!" It was Logan.

"We do, so get out of your car and help, will ya?" She grinned briefly as relief coursed through her. With Gunner and Renegade both on the chase, there was no way the kidnapper would escape. Their main objective was to keep the senator alive.

Logan stopped where he was and released Gunner from his car. They joined Caitlyn and Renegade, and she caught him up on the details of the situation, so far. Holding her blood-stained fingers out for Gunner to get Hyatt's scent, Caitlyn and her brother asked their dogs to track. Renegade, who had already picked up on the odor before Logan got there, took the lead. He ran down the tarmac, passing the row of hangars altogether. Gunner kept pace at his shoulder.

"They've got something!" Caitlyn yelled as she and Logan bolted after them.

The dogs led them to an equipment shed on the side of a pair of brick buildings. A shot rang out, and a bullet sparked against the pavement near Logan's feet. Caitlyn dashed for cover behind the last hangar to her right. Logan sprinted toward a maintenance truck parked on his left. He dove, tucking and rolling on the ground before coming to his knees ready to return fire. Shots rained down on him. Logan was trapped.

Caitlyn had a better angle. She took a second to assess where the gunfire came from. There were three shooters. The kidnapper had a team. A shiver of adrenaline skittered across her shoulders and down her spine. She and her brother were lucky to be alive. So were their dogs. Caitlyn sucked in a deep breath, held it, and pivoted around the corner of the hangar. Taking aim, she fired. Immediately, she swiveled back, pressing her shoulder blades to the wall.

A man screamed. Peering around the corner, she noted him face down on the ground and then she found her next target on the roof of the shed. Pivot, aim, fire! "Two down!"

The third shooter crept along the side of the small building. Caitlyn could barely see his silhouette, but she didn't have a clear shot. Renegade, however, did. He lunged from the shadows of the hangar they were hiding behind and flew across the pavement like a rocket. He launched himself the last twelve feet. His powerful jaws clamped down on the man's extended arm. His gun clattered to the ground as he shrieked in pain. Renegade's momentum knocked the man to the ground where he tugged on his target's arm, tearing into his flesh. Gunner joined Renegade at the shed. Barking, he scratched frantically at the door.

Caitlyn motioned to Logan that they were clear, and they both ran cautiously toward the building. She got to the man Renegade held and pressed her knee into his back. Handcuffing his free wrist, she said, "Good boy, Renegade! *Pust*. Let him go, buddy. I've got him." Instead of releasing him instantly, Ren shook his head causing his captive more pain. "Renegade, *Pust*!" When he still refused to release the man, Caitlyn reached down to her dog's fierce teeth and manually pulled his grip apart. Renegade, never inclined to release anyone who put her in danger, finally let him go when she physically insisted.

However, Renegade had not finished intimidating his captor. He stood, baring his bloody fangs, and growled at the man. "Good boy, Ren. *Zustan*. Hold him there."

Caitlyn caught up to Logan as he pried open the shed door. Gunner nosed his way inside, barking at his find. On a chair in the center of the room sat Senator Hyatt with two bricks of C4 that had been hastily duct-taped to his chest. The normally distinguished man cried. Tears and snot mingled together, running down his face. He had urinated himself, and it pooled on the floor underneath him. Caitlyn's mind hurled back to the day her first partner, Sam Dillinger, had died. A federal judge in Wyoming was the targeted victim of a bomb, and he and Sam were blown up. She blinked away the painful memories and focused on the explosive situation before her.

Logan crouched before the senator and studied the deadly apparatus. The C4 was the same as they'd seen before, but there was no timer attached to it. "Don't worry, sir. We're going to get you out of this." He turned to meet Caitlyn's hard gaze. His voice was gentle. "Catie-did, take the dogs and get out of here. Get the perp you cuffed and yourselves to a safe distance. Call Addison. I think she can tap into my body-cam and help me dismantle this bomb."

"No way, Logan. I wasn't there for Sam, and I will always regret it. There's no way I'm leaving you."

Her brother stared at her. His jaw muscles rippled. "I know how stubborn you can be, Cait, but now is not the time. You have to think about the little one you're carrying. In a choice between doing two right things, you must choose your baby first."

Caitlyn felt as though he'd slapped her hard. In the heat of the moment, she hadn't even thought about being pregnant. Instinct had taken over. Steel bands tightened around her heart. She was already proving to be a horrible mother. Tears heated her eyes and she blinked against them. They came both for her shame and for the risk she knew she had to allow her beloved brother to take in her place. "You're right... I'll go. But please, Logan. Be careful. Wait for Addison to help you. I'll call her as soon as we are at a safe distance."

"Good." Dark eyes that matched her own looked into her soul. "I love you, Caitlyn."

She swallowed the sudden lump in her throat. "Don't start that, Logan Reed. We know we love each other, but you better walk away from this, do you hear me?"

A ghost of a smile curled the edge of his mouth. "Roger that. Now get Gunner out of here."

Caitlyn knew Logan was remembering his own painful history—the day an explosion in Afghanistan killed his Army K9, Lobo. "I'll keep him safe, Log. I promise." She reached out and touched his cheek. "Gunner, *kemne.*"

Confused, Logan's dog looked to him for direction. "Go on, Gun. I'll be right out. Go!"

Caitlyn held the door for Gunner, and they left the shed together. She pulled the man Renegade was guarding to his feet. "Let's go."

"Your partner and Senator Hyatt will never get out of that shed alive," the man sneered.

Caitlyn shoved his back. "Get going, unless you want me to leave you cuffed to the side of the building."

The man stumbled forward, and Caitlyn followed him, flanked by the two dogs. SWAT officers took the man into custody and helped her connect to Addison through their comms. She described the situation, and Addison explained it was too risky to talk with Logan over a two-way radio or cell phone. "Radio signals can detonate bombs like this. I need you to make sure everyone moves away from the site by a minimum of 300 feet. Tell Logan I'm on my way. ETA thirteen minutes."

"Got it." Caitlyn held her breath before releasing it in a huff. Thirteen minutes was a lifetime. She prayed they had it. "Okay, Commander, we need you to get your people back 300 feet or more from that shed."

The SWAT commander ordered his officers to move. Two FBI agents accompanied the remaining shooter in an ambulance on his way to Sky Ridge Hospital to have his shredded arm attended to. Hopefully, the agents would get information out of him about the men responsible for all the bombs.

A huge engine growled as the FBI Bomb Squad's tactical vehicle screeched around the corner and drove straight toward her. It screeched to a halt. The back door swung open, and Addison jumped down already wearing her heavy bomb suit.

Caitlyn took Renegade and Gunner to stand behind the safety of the truck. It killed her not to be the one by Logan's side, but she would honor his request to keep his dog safe. She and her sister-in-law made eye contact, holding it long enough to communicate their mutual fear. Addison turned and slowly made her way to the shed where Logan and the senator waited. Their lives teetering on the reliability and strength of a bomb trigger.

Caitlyn felt utterly helpless and desperately wanted to be with Logan. She thought of Colt, wishing she could hear his calm, confident voice. It was around four in the morning. She told herself that she would talk to him soon. She would call her husband when Logan was safe and this whole nightmare was over. Until then, she buried her face in Renegade's neck, and he nuzzled her cheek, sensing her anxiety.

27

Logan breathed a little easier knowing that Gunner had left with Caitlyn. He couldn't handle it if an explosion took another of his dogs. Lobo's face loomed in his mind's eye, and his heart swelled with the memories—both heartwarming and painful—and with gratitude toward Gunner, who had helped him heal from his loss. Caitlyn would take care of his dog if things didn't go as he hoped with the bomb. The assurance gave him confidence to focus on the job he needed to do.

"Do you know how to get me out of this thing?" Senator Hyatt's voice jolted Logan out of his reverie. The senator held up a rectangular device in his fist. His thumb pressed a red button on the end of it. "The man who taped all this to me said when I let go of this button, I'll blow to kingdom come." Sweat dripped from Hyatt's drenched silver hair that was matted to his head. Large damp stains circled the underarms of his high-dollar, pinstriped dress shirt. "My hand aches already. I don't know how long I can hold on."

"Okay. Hang in there for a little longer. If I can't find something to help, I'll help hold the button down myself." Logan looked around the shed for something he could use. A closet contained brooms, shovels, and a hose. Nothing in there. On a single shelf sat a variety of tools and boxes filled with nails and screws. Hanging from the pegboard backing was a long peg that was poking through three rolls of tape. Bingo! Logan tossed the masking tape and grabbed the roll of duct tape. He wrapped a long strip several times around the senator's hand, holding his thumb tight against the trigger. "Now you can relax. Don't worry. The best bomb tech in Denver will be here in just a few minutes. Her name is Addison, and she can dismantle anything. I'm not leaving you and we're both going to be okay." Even as he spoke the comforting words, sweat trickled down Logan's forehead into his brows. He pressed the pad on the side of the mic attached to his protective vest. "Is she here yet?"

"Your wife... Agent Reed, I mean... ordered no radio communication from here on out. But she just arrived and is on her way to your location." Logan didn't bother to end the call. He shouldn't have made it in the first place.

Instead, he engaged the senator, more to keep him calm than anything. "Do you know who the men are who did this to you? Why are they targeting you?"

"Not these men specifically, but I know who sent them. The bastard's name is Ted Marrin. He leads a special ecological interest group called the Sovereign Earth Alliance. It's a radical eco-liberal faction with revolutionary overtones. They're troublemakers."

"That's who the FBI suspected. What do they stand for?"

"Their focus is on land, constitutional rights, and the decentralization of power."

"How do you know it was them?"

"Because Marrin warned me that something like this would happen if I didn't listen to him and cave to his demands."

"Did you report the warning to your security staff?"

"Agent, do you have any idea how many threats a senator gets on a given day? I didn't take him seriously. Obviously, I should have."

"What do they have against you?"

"I am developing a wilderness area south of Westcliffe. It's out in the middle of nowhere. My investors and I are building a southern Colorado ski resort that will rival Vail and Aspen."

Cutting off further discussion, the call of a familiar voice brought relief to the vise-like tension in Logan's neck and shoulders. He let out a breath he didn't realize he'd been holding. "The bomb tech is here. We're alright now."

"Thank God!"

"I'm coming in." Addison pulled open the door to the shed and shuffled in. Her protective bomb suit made it difficult for her to get through the narrow opening and Logan took her hand to pull her in.

"Hey, gorgeous." Logan made room for her, torn between relief and abject fear that she was going to attempt to dismantle the bomb.

Addison smiled at him through the clear visor of her helmet and shook her head. "Does this outfit make my butt look big?" Logan forced a laugh, grateful for the comedic relief though it didn't really work. Anxiety continued to claw up his insides. "Show me what we've got."

Logan described how the kidnappers had hastily created a makeshift explosive vest by taping two bricks of C4 to the senator's chest. "There are wires connecting the two chunks, but I don't see any timing device."

"Then there must be a detonator somewhere else."

"Yeah, they gave a hand-held to the senator. It's the kind with a pressure button. If he lets go, the bomb will explode. He was losing his grip, so I taped his thumb down to it so he can relax his fingers while the trip mechanism remains engaged."

"Good thinking. That buys us some time." Addison peered at the wires stuck into the C4. "Logan, you need to leave. Go back to the truck and have the team deploy the containment vessel. I want this C4 inside it and far away before I unwrap Senator Hyatt's hand."

"But—"

"No buts, Reed. That's an order."

Logan's chest deflated. Everything in his body and soul told him to stay with her. To protect her.

Adisson arched an elegantly shaped black eyebrow and gave him her no-nonsense glare. "Logan?"

He sighed. "Yes, Ma'am." He gripped her forearm.

"Please be careful." He touched the clear visor of Addison's helmet with his fingertips.

She made a kissing motion with her lips. "I always am. Now, go. You can watch the procedure on the monitor."

Releasing another gush of tension, Logan exited the small building and jogged toward The Beast. Finding Caitlyn and the dogs behind the vehicle, he gestured for them to follow him inside where they could see what Addison was doing in the shed. A large part of him didn't want to watch his wife as she took apart a bomb. But he couldn't avoid it, either. "Guys, Agent Reed wants the containment vessel deployed," he told the techs when they climbed aboard.

"Roger that." An agent seated before a large monitor pressed several keys on his keyboard and then picked up a joystick to steer the heavy round ball on wheels.

Logan pointed Caitlyn to the screen. "That sphere of steel has twelve-inch-thick walls and can handle up to ten pounds of explosives." They leaned over the technician's shoulders at a real-time black and white video of the vessel as it rolled toward the shed.

Another monitor displayed the live feed from Addison's body cam. Her hands were steady as she skillfully cut the tape on the senator's torso. Logan continually reminded himself to breathe as his wife carefully placed the bricks of C4 inside the containment vessel, wires and all. She locked it tight and gave her team a thumbs up.

"Let's roll this baby out to the runway, in case she blows." The tech with the joystick maneuvered the explosives as far away from them as he could. Addison waited until he gave the go-ahead over the now usable radio.

She pulled a small knife from her utility belt and slowly cut the thick tape from the senator's hand. The second she released his thumb from the pressure button, an explosion shook the ground. Logan gripped the back of the chair he stood behind for support. Caitlyn dropped to a knee and wrapped her arm around Renegade.

Logan's gaze shot to the screen depicting the blown-apart containment vessel, and his mouth dropped open. The heavy lid had been blown open and fell back, perched off- kilter on top of the base like a jaunty hat. The warped and twisted hinge and locking mechanism stuck out at unnatural angles. The container's wheels had blown off, and though the sphere had done its job, it was destroyed in the process.

Logan jumped out of the Beast and ran to meet Addison as she escorted Senator Hyatt from the shed. The scent of burning metal, resembling gunpowder mixed with melted plastic, hung in the air. The legislator's legs wobbled, and he stumbled as EMTs met him with a stretcher.

Addison unclipped her helmet. "I hope that's the last bomb you're planning on finding tonight, Mister. I'm exhausted."

Logan swept her up, 90-pound bomb suit and all, and spun her around. "Let's get you home."

"Yes, please." She awkwardly kissed Logan despite the bulky suit. "But first, get me out of this thing." Turning, she grinned at Caitlyn. "I'd say we've had a successful night, don't you think? Let's let Sanchez and his team sort through all the pieces and clean up this mess. I vote we swing by McDonald's and grab a bagful of egg and biscuit sandwiches. Then I'm hitting the hay. I'm completely whacked."

"You're on! I'm buying." Caitlyn laughed releasing all the stress of the evening. Renegade wagged his tail and barked at them. "Don't worry, boy. You'll get one, too."

28

Colt escorted the mayor to the door. "Thanks for stopping by Barry, but I had better get back to work. We have a lot going on right now."

"Okay, but think about how nice it would be to have an admin officer, Sheriff. The extra money a housing development would bring into Moose Creek would help all of us, and I would be sure to set aside a healthy amount for your department."

"Barry, there is no way Dylan Reed is selling any part of his land to some citified outsider, and you know it. Find Dray some other property to look at."

"But... it's the Reed property and a few others along the river that Dray is interested in," Mayor Ringleman sputtered. "Riverside property would sell at a premium."

Gears clicked into place in Colt's mind. "Properties like the Colwell place and Beyer's ranch?"

"I suppose so, yes." Ringleman's eyes shifted nervously.

"You wouldn't know anything about recent vandalism

on those ranches, would you? Like someone killing Dylan's cows? Or burning buildings and wrecking gates? These are mighty big coincidences."

"What are you talking about? I don't know anything of the sort. The nerve!" Ringleman puffed himself up in a huff and then his mouth twitched as he regarded Colt. "What do you mean by 'big coincidences?'"

"The same properties your developer friend is interested in are the ones that were recently vandalized. If I find out that Mason Dray is trying to intimidate Moose Creek ranchers into selling their property, he'll end up in jail."

"Hmph! I'm sure I don't know what you're talking about. Dray has no need for intimidation tactics. He has a ton of money to offer instead."

"I hope you're right. But I will find out either way. And you should tell him I said so." Colt opened the door and the mayor stormed out. It would be almost impossible to prove that Dray vandalized those properties, but hopefully the threat of being investigated would bring the damage to an end.

Colt's phone rang, and he crossed the office to answer it. "Branson here... I mean Moose Creek County Sheriff's Department."

"Colt, it's Blake Kennedy here. I'm calling about the young woman you recently found in the mountains. Jessica Alcott?"

"Yes, is she okay?"

"She will be. However, I want to keep her at the hospital overnight. She's suffering from exposure and dehydration. And honestly, she's very upset over being held in the cabin with a seriously injured man whom she was unable to help. I'd like her to see a therapist in the morning and get her set up with follow-up care at home. Her parents are on their way here from Wisconsin."

"Is it alright with you if I stop by to ask her a few questions tonight before I head home?"

"It's kind of late."

"I'll keep it short. I think the man she's referring to is a missing hunter we've been searching for. If she has any information that can help us find him, it could save his life." Colt banked on Blake caving to the thought of saving someone's life.

"I suppose, then. But only a few questions. She is already exhausted from her experience up there."

"I promise. I'll head over as soon as I close up shop here."

Thinking about Jessica reminded Colt of the SIM card he had removed from her drone. He pulled it from his pocket, inserted it into a slot on his computer, and pressed play on the video file. A panoramic view of the mountain and adjacent valley filled his screen. The scene played out like the prelude to a grand western, with hills and trees moving past. All it needed was the music.

Soon the video-scape narrowed and focused on the mine entrance. Jessica took several still images from different angles. The view broadened again, and the cabin came into view. Jessica must have seen it and directed the drone to move in closer. In the top right corner of Colt's laptop, he glimpsed what he thought was a second cabin, but then the screen fritzed and went blank. A bullet had ended the taping.

Colt leaned back in his chair. *What was it they didn't want her to see?* He watched the video again before he turned off his computer for the night. On his way out, he grabbed his jacket and hat, flipped off the lights, and locked the office door behind him.

He quietly knocked on the door of Jessica's hospital room. "Jessica? It's Sheriff Branson. How are you feeling?"

"Much better, thanks. Doctor Blake fixed me up with an IV." The young woman blushed when she said Kennedy's name, and Colt did an inner eye roll. Every woman he knew swooned for that guy. Kennedy could have any female he wanted, but his heart belonged to Colt's wife. He refused to let his mind travel down that path too far. Caitlyn had set the doctor up with a friend of hers who lived in Billings. With any luck at all, their relationship would work out and Colt could stop worrying about his own.

"Good. He said you were a little dehydrated. Listen, I have a few quick questions for you, if you feel up to it."

"Sure." Jessica pushed herself up against her pillows.

Colt removed his cowboy hat. "I'd like to talk about the man who was in the cabin with you. Can you describe his injuries?"

Her face closed. "Not really. He remained balled up on the floor for the most part. He never spoke to me."

"Was he bleeding?"

"Yes, I think so. I mean, his clothes were bloody. I don't know if he was still bleeding while he lay there. I really hope not." Tears filled her eyes.

"Did he say anything? Make any noise?"

"Maybe. He groaned a lot. I think he might have said, 'Help me' but I can't be sure."

Colt took it as good news that the man was at least alive when Jessica last saw him. With any luck, he still would be when they found him. "Could you tell roughly how old the man was?"

"Probably about my dad's age, I guess. Forty-five to fifty."

Colt scrolled on his phone to the missing hunter's photo and showed it to Jessica. "Is this the man?"

She gasped and covered her mouth with her hand. "I... I think... I guess so. It seems like it might be him."

"Thanks, Jessica. You've been a great help. Now, get a good night's rest. Feel better in the morning."

Colt left buoyed by the hope that Paul Sandlewood was still alive. It was almost eleven o'clock by the time he got home. It had been a long day, and he was exhausted. Without turning on the light, he went to the garage, opened the kennel door, and scooped some dog food into Storm's bowl. He trudged from there to the cabin and went straight to bed. He kicked off his boots, unbuckled his belt, and pulled off his jeans. Looking forward to sleeping in a little longer than usual the following morning, he crawled under the covers and crashed.

29

———

Colt had planned to sleep in for at least an additional half hour. The house was quiet with only him, and he'd had a late night the night before. But when his phone rang at 6:30am, his hope for a few extra Zs was dashed. Grumbling, he fumbled in the dark room for the device, which clanged loudly from his nightstand. "Hello?" Colt cleared his throat and swiped at his eyes. "Sheriff Branson, here."

"Is Jace with you?"

Colt pushed himself up and swung his legs over the side of the bed. "Allison? What are you talking about?"

"Is. Jace. With. You?" she repeated.

"No. Of course not. You picked him up yesterday. What's going on?" Colt's nervous system hummed on alert bringing him to full attention.

"I went to wake Jace for school this morning, but he wasn't in his bed. His bed hadn't even been slept in!" Allison's high-pitched words teetered on hysteria.

"Okay, calm down. Did you look everywhere in the house? The yard?"

"Of course I did. I'm not an idiot. He's not here, Colt!"

"Have you called any of his friends?"

"I don't have their numbers."

Colt ran his hand over his face and kneaded the back of his neck. "I'll call a few of his friends and check in with Dylan. He went out to the ranch the last time he pulled a stunt like this."

"I told you so! That ranch causes nothing but trouble."

"Allison, can we at least wait until we find him before you start blaming me?" Colt kept the fact that she was the one who lost their son this time to himself. "I'll put Wes and Izzy on the alert too. They can start looking around town. Keep your phone with you in case Jace tries to contact you. Remember he doesn't have his phone anymore, so answer every call even if you don't recognize the number." With that, Colt hung up.

His first move was to call Dylan. "Jace isn't out there again, is he?"

"No. I don't think so. I haven't been out to the barn yet, though. I'll go look for any signs of him and call you back in a few minutes."

Colt ran through the list of Jace's three closest school friends. No one had seen or heard from him. He called Wes at the office. "Jace is missing. He's been testing out his independence a lot lately. I'm hoping he just left Allison's house early and is wandering around town before school. Will you and Izzy make the rounds? See if you can find him? I'm going to drive out to the Reeds' ranch and look for him there."

"Sure thing, boss. I'll let you know if we see any sign of him."

Colt threw on yesterday's jeans under his wrinkled work shirt and pulled on his boots. He skipped coffee and breakfast as he jogged out to his Jeep. Crossing the yard, he noticed the garage door was partially open. Could Jace be in there? It made no sense, but he checked anyway.

He pushed open the door. "Jace?" The small unattached garage was crowded with storage boxes, tools, and miscellany, but a quick glance around told him no one was there. He scanned the space more slowly. Something was out of place. Storm was not in his kennel. It took Colt two more passes to realize that several items from his camping gear were missing as well. Most obvious was his backpack, which he kept hung by the frame on the wall. It was gone. He looked closer and saw that his tent and sleeping bag had also disappeared.

Colt returned to the cabin to gain optimal phone coverage and called Allison. "I think Jace has run away. My backpacking gear is missing."

"Where would he go? Can you find him?" Fear had replaced her incriminations for now, and Colt wanted to reassure her.

"I will find him. I imagine he's somewhere on the ranch property. Dylan is looking now, but I'm headed out there to join him."

"But how would Jace get all the way to your house to gather the gear and then carry it over to the Reeds?"

"I'm not sure." Colt didn't want to add to Allison's

worry by telling her Jace probably hitch-hiked. "I'll call you as soon as I know anything."

He phoned Dylan and Wes to relay the new information before he sprinted out to his car. Once he was on the highway, he dialed Caitlyn.

"H-lo?" His wife's sleepy voice cracked. "Colt?"

"Hey, babe. Sorry to call so early, but Jace is missing."

"What?" Caitlyn's voice was suddenly clear and strong. "How long has he been gone? Where did you last see him?"

"He left Allison's house at some point last night after dinner. She didn't realize he was missing until this morning when she went to wake him for school. The alarming thing is, my backpacking gear is gone, too. That means he somehow came home to get that before he took off again."

"So, he ran away?"

"Looks that way. I'm headed out to the ranch now. That's my best guess for where to start looking."

"Did he take Storm with him?"

"He must have."

"Well, that's at least one good thing. Be sure to take Jace's jacket or something with you that McKenzie can use for Athena to track his scent."

"Good idea. Maybe he left a sweatshirt or something at the ranch."

"I'll be on the next flight home."

Colt's chest expanded with warmth. "Thanks, but you don't have to do that. We'll probably find him in no time."

"I hope so, but either way, I'm coming home. Jace

needs us right now, and that's all that matters. I love you. I'll see you soon."

Colt flipped on his red and blue lights and the siren. He blazed his way through Moose Creek and out the other side on the mountain highway toward the ranch. He arrived to see four horses tacked and ready to go hitched to the post outside the barn. Dylan and John checked cinches while McKenzie held an old T-shirt of Jace's for Athena to smell. Stella held baby Rose in one arm as she passed out breakfast sandwiches to everyone.

After parking his car, Colt jogged to Stella, accepted his breakfast to-go and kissed his mother-in-law on the cheek. "Thanks, Stella. Call my satellite phone if you hear anything from Jace." He crossed the barnyard and climbed onto Whiskey's back.

McKenzie held the shirt for Athena to smell and then stuffed it into a saddlebag before she mounted her mare. "Ready, everyone? Athena, find him! Find Jace!" Athena scampered around the barnyard until she caught a scent and took off on the trail that skirted the arena, passed by the old tree swing and meandered up the mountain. McKenzie trotted after her dog, leaving Colt, Dylan, and John to follow.

30

Caitlyn jumped out of her bed, dashed down the hall, and burst into Logan and Addison's room. "Logan! Jace ran away. I have to get home as fast as I can."

Logan peered up at her through eyes barely open. His dark hair stood on end. "What time is it?" His voice was scratchy and weak.

"Early. I know you've hardly slept, but I need your help. Meet me downstairs." She ran back to the guest room. After throwing on some jeans and a T-shirt, Caitlyn jammed the rest of her clothes into her duffel bag. Renegade bounced up and down in response to her agitated energy. Together they rumbled down the stairs and into the kitchen, where she hastily fed her dog and made a strong pot of coffee.

A minute later, Logan, who had dressed in an old Army sweatshirt and black athletic shorts, plodded into the room. He was on the phone but nodded thanks when

Caitlyn handed him some fresh coffee in a to-go tumbler. She placed her hands on his shoulders and turned him toward the living room, guiding him to the front door. Addison and Gunner met them there.

Logan leaned over to kiss his wife. "Be back soon."

Caitlyn stroked Gunner's head and hugged her sleepy sister-in-law as they left. "Thanks for letting me stay with you guys last week. I'll call you when I hear anything about Jace."

"Please do. I know you'll find him but keep us posted until you do." Addison waved them off as Logan drove away with Caitlyn and Renegade.

"You're in luck." The coffee and cool morning air had revived Logan's voice. "I called Cameron to see if we could use the FBI jet to get you home. He said he had already scheduled a flight up to Wyoming today with some ATF and Homeland agents on an ATF helicopter. Apparently, Colt talked with Sanchez yesterday about the explosive materials and other items he found in the caves, and they want to interview the surveyors and view the potential evidence for themselves. They've agreed to leave early and to give you and Renegade a ride. Addison and I will drive your car up this weekend. Will that be soon enough?"

Caitlyn reached across the console and threw her arms around her brother's neck, causing him to swerve. "You're the best!"

Logan straightened the car in the lane and brushed at the coffee that had spilled from his mug onto his lap. "Hey, watch it, crazy woman. You're going to make me crash." His chastisement came with an indulgent grin.

. . .

COLT AND DYLAN met the ATF helicopter, which landed in the northern pasture at the ranch. Caitlyn and Renegade were the first ones out of the craft. She jumped into Colt's arms. "Have you found Jace yet?"

Colt held her tight, shaking his head. She could tell he was barely holding it together. Worry for his son had overwhelmed him.

"We will." She pulled back and looked him in the eye. "Renegade *will* find him. I promise."

Wes arrived with Izzy to meet with the federal agents. They brought the suspicious items with them, minus the C4, which Colt had sent off with the WBI for safekeeping.

Caitlyn gave Dylan a quick hug. "Can Colt and I borrow your truck?"

"Sure, but I thought you'd want to go out and look for Jace right away." Dylan's eyes narrowed at her in question.

"I do. But I want to start at our garage. We'll be able to determine where Jace went after he took Colt's gear. We'll know it if he got into a car because his trail will end on the road. If that's the case, searching the ranch makes sense. But if he didn't, then we're looking in the wrong place. I've been thinking about it, if Jace took Storm with him, it isn't very likely that he hitched a ride. I mean, who would pick up a kid and a pit bull?"

Colt closed his eyes, and his shoulders slumped in self-reproach. "I didn't think about that. I just figured..."

"You can't worry about that. It was as good a guess as any. But since Athena hasn't found Jace on the ranch yet, we may as well look somewhere else, too." She clasped her husband's hand. His calloused fingers were ice cold in hers. "None of this is your fault, Colt, and we're going to find him."

He swallowed hard and nodded as they jogged to Dylan's truck. Caitlyn opened the back door and told Ren to load up. In one fluid movement, her dog sprang into the crew cab and sat, panting on the seat, ready to go.

When they got home, Colt ran inside to grab one of Jace's shirts for Renegade to smell. Caitlyn and Renegade went straight to the garage. Ren whined when Colt held Jace's shirt to his nose.

"*Stopa*, Ren. Find Jace!" Caitlyn commanded. Renegade barked several times and then went to work. In seconds, he found a fresh trail and took off. Caitlyn and Colt ran after him. Ren darted to the back of the property, where Jace's scent led them into the surrounding woods.

Renegade bolted ahead, and Caitlyn, exhausted from the night before and running on too little sleep, had a difficult time keeping up with him. "Ren! Wait up!" When she and Colt caught up with him, she attached a long tether to his vest. Stopping to catch her breath, she peered up at Colt. "Ren is on Jace's trail. As far as I know, Jace has never hiked up this way. Have you come this way with him before?

"No. We've only hiked together on the ranch."

"Okay. Don't worry, we're going to find him soon."

Colt swept a strand of her hair behind her ear. "Thanks for coming home, Catie. For doing this. It means everything to me."

"Of course, Colt. There's no way I could stay in Denver with our son lost in the woods. Nothing is more important than finding him."

Colt stilled. The clouds left his eyes and his face brightened. "You said, 'our son.'"

Caitlyn smiled up at him. "That's who he is, isn't he?"

Colt pulled her into a suffocating hug. She enjoyed the closeness for a quick moment before she pushed back. "Plenty of time for that, but let's get going. I'm texting Dylan to let him know Renegade has found Jace's trail. Then, we can go find him."

Two hours and almost ten miles later, Renegade led them to a small, rugged campsite complete with a poorly constructed tent and a ring of stones surrounding black ashes. But neither Jace nor Storm were there.

"This is my gear, but where is Jace?" Colt held his hand over the fire pit. "It's cold." He turned in a circle, shouting out Jace's name several times.

Caitlyn joined in calling for the boy while she peeked inside the tent. "Your backpack is in here. Maybe he's out hunting for lunch."

Startling them, Renegade barked in a frantic high alert. Caitlyn sprinted to where he was pointing toward a small clearing behind a hedge of scrub oak. She pushed past the shrubs and stopped dead in her tracks. "Colt!" she yelled.

Colt rushed to her side, and together they stared at the sight lying on a bed of straw before them. It was Storm. His light gray form curled into itself. He didn't lift his head at their arrival. He didn't move at all. Caitlyn dropped to her knees next to him and felt his body. He was warm, and a weak but steady pulse beat against her fingers. Noticing a red-tufted dart dangling from his hip, she called out, "Storm's alive! He's breathing. I think he's been tranquilized."

"Who would do that to him?" Colt's voice tightened with fear. "Where is Jace?"

Caitlyn swallowed hard. She had no answers to give her husband.

Colt retrieved the sleeping bag while Caitlyn gently removed the dart. Together they rolled Storm onto the blanket and carried him to the tent. "Whoever did this wanted to keep Storm out of the way." She didn't add the rest of her thought, which was that whoever it was did it so they could get to Jace. She scanned the campsite with a sharper gaze, looking for signs of a struggle, desperate to find their son. Jace may have started out by running away from home, but it was clear he was running from someone else, too.

"Now that I'm looking at this campsite with a fresh perspective, I think there was a scuffle here." Colt pulled at a droopy corner of the tent. "My first thought was that Jace simply didn't do a good job setting things up, but that's not like him. He takes pride in how well he can make camp." Colt's voice rose in fear at the end of his sentence. He cleared his throat and took a deep stabilizing breath.

Caitlyn gripped his arm and he tried to draw comfort

from her. "I agree. And look over there, behind the tent. His cooking pot is face down in the dirt. He wouldn't leave it there like that. And listen, it's a good sign that whoever tranquilized Storm didn't intend to hurt him." Renegade continued to sniff around the camp, and seconds later, he bolted off into the surrounding trees. "Ren found Jace's trail again. Let's go!"

Colt followed Caitlyn and Renegade into the forest, which in some places grew so thick it blocked out the daylight. A sick feeling clawed its way up Colt's throat even as they tracked Jace. They ran forward, into the fear of what they might discover. *Was Jace kidnapped? Or was he running from Storm's attacker? Would they find him in time to save him from danger?*

Occasionally, Renegade paused and sniffed in a circle before darting off in an unexpected direction. After several more miles, they stopped to drink some water and give themselves and Renegade a brief break. They sat in the silence of their own thoughts. Ren's ears perked forward, and he jumped to all fours.

Caitlyn sat taller in response to her dog, listening for what had caused him to alert. "What is it, Ren? Do you hear Jace?" Renegade lowered his head. A guttural growl rumbled from his chest and throat. "*Stopa*, Ren! Find Jace! Go!" Caitlyn stuffed her water bottle into its holder on her belt and bolted after him.

Goosebumps rose over the surface of Colt's skin. He didn't like the sound of Renegade's growl. With automatic precision, he checked the magazine in his gun, snapping it back in place as he ran behind Caitlyn.

As they got nearer Renegade's target, voices echoed

under the canopy of pines. Caitlyn held a finger to her lips before she climbed a rock formation that her dog had already crested. Colt was right on her heels. Together, they peered over the top of the stones to a clearing below on the other side.

Jace was there!

His son was tied to a tree, and blood was smeared from his nose across his face. Two men stood before him. One had a slight build and dark, slicked-back hair. He wore brand new clothing that looked like it had come off the rack at REI that morning. The other, a thicker man, was dressed in worn jeans and an old Carhartt jacket. Behind them blazed a campfire they had lit on the ground without bothering to contain it in a stone circle.

It was the second guy that Colt focused on. He watched in horror as the stout man lifted a burning stick from the fire and thrust the flaming end toward Jace's face. "Tell us where our stuff is."

Jace raised his chin, bravely trying not to cry. "I don't know anything about your stuff. What stuff? All I did was take pictures of you guys, and then you wrecked my phone, so I don't even have that."

The red-hot poker flew closer to Jace's face, and Colt surged forward, stopped only by Caitlyn's firm grasp. It was a fourteen-foot drop from where they were. There was no way to help Jace from where they were without being seen and perhaps putting him in worse danger than he already was.

Renegade watched Caitlyn's every move. He stared directly into her eyes, waiting for her command. Finally, she pointed and gave him a sharp nod. Renegade sprang from his perch on the rocks down to the forest floor below. In one stride he threw himself against the man who threatened Jace. He knocked him off his feet and clamped down on his upper arm. The guy screamed in pain.

"Let's go, Colt!" Caitlyn skidded down the boulders on her backside and ran around the rocks into the clearing. Renegade had the burly man subdued, but his leaner partner had drawn a pistol and aimed it at Jace.

"Stop right there. Call off your dog, or I'll shoot the kid."

"Renegade, *pust!*" Responding to the fear in Caitlyn's voice, Renegade released the man's arm but remained in place growling over him. "What's going on here? What do you guys want with an eleven-year-old boy?"

"He stole something from me, and I want it back," the dark-haired man spat.

"What does he have?"

"He knows."

Jace who had at first looked relieved to see them, now blinked back tears, valiantly working to appear brave. "I don't have anything. I saw some men on Uncle Dylan's land, and I took some pictures. They caught me and smashed my phone. That's all!"

"Shut up, kid." The man backhanded Jace across the face. Renegade barked and growled with fury.

Colt didn't take a single second to think. He crashed across the clearing, spearing the man with his body, tackling him to the ground. The gun clattered against the rock wall. Caitlyn, who was right behind Colt, scooped it up. Pressing the slide, she dropped the magazine to the dirt and tossed the gun across the clearing into the underbrush. Swinging her arm back around, she gripped her own weapon and leveled it at the man whom Colt had pinned down.

"Cuff him, Colt. Then get the other guy." Caitlyn stepped sideways toward Jace, never taking her eyes off his attacker. "Jace, are you okay?"

"Yes, but they shot Storm!" His young voice broke then, and tears flowed down his face washing streaks through the blood on his cheeks.

"Storm is okay! We found him, buddy, and he's going to be alright." Caitlyn reassured Jace while she worked to untie him. Colt checked the two men for more weapons. He then bound them together, back-to-back. He ran to Jace and knelt before him, checking the boy's bloody face. His fingers trembled as they ran over his battered skin. Colt kissed his son's forehead. As soon as Caitlyn had Jace completely free, he wrapped his arms around the boy's thin shoulders. "I've been so worried about you." Colt's heart hammered so hard it hurt.

Jace slung his thin arms tight around Colt's neck. "I knew you'd find me, Dad! I knew it!"

"You didn't make it easy." Colt searched his son's eyes, which were just like his own. "If it weren't for Catie and Ren..." He shuddered. "I was with Aunt McKenzie and Athena earlier, but we were looking in the wrong place."

Jace beamed at Caitlyn while Renegade licked his hands and face. "I could never hide from Caitlyn and Ren."

Caitlyn hugged Jace to her chest. "Don't you ever run away again, do you hear me? If you have a problem, then we talk about it. I mean it, Jace. You scared your dad and me to death. Not to mention your mom and the rest of our family. You could have gotten killed out here." She kissed the top of his head hard three times.

Wiping the affection from his brow, Jace laughed and grinned up at her. "I'm sorry. I really am. I just wanted to prove I could make it on my own."

Caitlyn rested her hand on Jace's head, and Colt knelt next to him, gripping his narrow shoulders. "You *can't* make it on your own, son. None of us can. We're not meant to. It's why you have a family who loves you." He stood and ruffled Jace's hair. "We have a long hike back before we can put these men in jail. Do you think you can make it?"

"Yes, sir."

"Good. We can talk about all of this on the way."

Caitlyn pulled a plastic bag from her utility belt. She retrieved the gun she had thrown into the bushes and its magazine and stuffed them inside before she nudged their prisoners to their feet. "Why did you two follow Jace into the mountains?"

The smaller man glared at her with his beady eyes. "Because he stole something from us. He came home unexpectedly last night and when he tromped off into the forest, we followed him."

"What do you think he stole? And why were you out at our cabin?"

"We want our things back. Your little brat stole some maps and some other valuables from our cave, and we want them back."

"My son didn't take your things. I did." Colt prodded

the man's shoulder, causing the bound duo to stumble. "And it's not *your* cave."

"Let's go." Caitlyn stepped off. "We have some friends from the FBI who want to speak with you."

The dark-haired man's eyes shifted from her to Colt, widening in shock. "The FBI?"

31

Dylan, McKenzie, and Wes stood in the front yard of Colt and Caitlyn's cabin with Burke Cameron and two ATF agents waiting for them when they returned. Colt had messaged Dylan as soon as they found Jace, to let the family know he was safe and asked him to call an ambulance for the man Renegade had torn up. It had been a long, slow-going hike back home managing the two suspects, a hurting boy, and carrying a groggy dog.

Cameron took hold of the dark-haired suspect. "Theodore Marrin, you're under arrest for the—"

The man jerked violently from Burke's grasp. "Hold on! I'm not Theodore Marrin!"

Dylan strode to Cameron's side. "No, this guy's name is Mason Dray. The spineless developer who's been sneaking around town wreaking havoc hoping to frighten local ranchers into selling him their land."

Colt took custody of Dray from Cameron. "In that

case, you're under arrest for trespassing, vandalism and kidnapping. Wes, read this man his rights and take him to jail, and as soon as his partner gets stitched up, stick him in there too."

Cameron scratched his chin. "My boss sent me up here to arrest the ringleader of the Sovereign Earth Alliance. He said that you found C4 and a coded journal that belonged to Ted Marrin in a mountain cave. So where is he?"

Colt cinched his brows together. "We found those things along with the maps Dray was talking about, articles to make Molotov cocktails and a blueprint. I sent pictures of it all to Logan Reed, but I don't know anything about someone named Marrin."

"Right, and Reed sent the journal images to some code analysts. They discovered lists of explosives and guns, with buyers and costs. You were right about the blueprint, too. It was a page torn from a copy of the originals of DIA."

Colt rested his hands on his hips. "That's good. But we never found any evidence of firearms, and there was only a small amount of C4 along with the stuff for hand-made explosives."

Cocking her head, Caitlyn asked, "So, are Dray and Marrin connected somehow?"

Cameron shook his head and shrugged. "I don't know, but we're not leaving Wyoming until we get to the bottom of this. Mind if we use your office, Sheriff?"

"Not at all. You can follow my deputy into town and make yourselves at home." Colt clasped the back of Jace's neck. "But I'm going to take this guy inside and clean up his bloody nose." Colt shifted his attention to Jace. "We ought to get a cold pack on those bruises, too" He leaned down and peered at his son's face. "You're going to have another shiner, for sure." They turned to go inside the cabin when the sound of tires coming down the gravel drive caused him to turn. *Allison.*

Allison parked next to Dylan's truck and jumped out of her car. She ran to Jace, and cupping his chin, took in his battered face. "Thank God you're safe. Does it hurt terribly bad?"

"I'm okay." Jace pulled away from his mom's grasp.

"I can't believe you ran away. Do you have any idea how scared I was?"

Colt slid his arm protectively around Jace's shoulders. "We can discuss all that later. Right now, I want to get him cleaned up."

Caitlyn took Jace's hand. "I can do that. I'm sure you and Allison have a lot to talk about."

Allison crossed her arms over her chest and nodded. Colt accepted that they had much to discuss, though he'd rather do it another time. Relenting, he said, "Okay, thanks Catie." He gestured for Allison to take one of the chairs on the porch. He joined her in the other.

"I'm so relieved that you finally found him," she huffed.

Colt crossed an ankle over his knee. "Thanks to Caitlyn and Renegade."

"Yes. Well." She cast her gaze out to the yard.

"I think this experience was enough of a lesson on its own. I don't think we need to punish Jace any further. Though I do want to talk it all through with him."

A slight smile brushed her pink, glossy lips. Allison may have been worried about Jace, but she still took the time to make up her face and do her hair. She was a beautiful woman, but her efforts rang hollow, given the circumstances. "I'm sure you're right. You usually are."

Colt had expected an argument or at least a rant about their son, and an accusation of how Colt was somehow to blame for everything. Stunned by her acquiescence, he set his boot on the deck and leaned forward. Bracing his forearms on his knees, he stared at her.

"The thing is," she sighed. "I am simply not able to deal with that boy. He's too much for me."

Jace chose that moment to dash out the door with Storm and Renegade chasing after him. Allison jumped at the sound of the door slamming behind them and pressed her hand against her chest.

"Hey!" Colt called. "Shouldn't you be resting?"

"Caitlyn said as long as my head didn't hurt, I could play with the dogs." Jace waved and then threw a ball for Renegade and Storm to retrieve.

Allison shook her head. "See? I would have yelled at him and sent him to his room. Which he would have resented, and then he wouldn't have talked to me for the rest of the day."

"We will speak to him about his behavior, but he needs a little time before we process this whole thing. It's not just the running away, but also the skipping school. I think Jace is struggling to figure out where he belongs. We need to be firm but also patient with him. Eleven is a tough age anyway but having to switch back and forth between our houses is upsetting, and I imagine he's worried about how he'll fit in when the baby gets here."

"You will all make a really nice family." Absent was the sarcasm Colt expected to accompany such a comment. Instead, Allison sounded wistful.

"We'll work all this out together," he responded tentatively, unsure of her mood.

Allison sat quietly for several minutes, watching Jace play. When she finally spoke, her voice was soft. "The truth is, Colt, I hate living in Moose Creek, but Jace pitches an all-out war whenever I talk about the possibility of moving." She turned to face him, her expression earnest. "I have an amazing job offer as an office manager at a mega car dealership back in Missouri, and I'd really like to take it."

Colt swallowed and sat perfectly still. If Allison was planning on taking Jace away from him, he would never let that happen. He'd fight it all the way. He'd come to love his son so deeply over the short time he'd known him. He could no longer imagine his life without Jace in it every day.

"But the new job would mean long hours," Allison continued. "And I already can't seem to handle Jace. The thing is, I can't see a way to accept the job and make it work with him."

Colt saw an opening and quietly leaned in. "What if you let Jace stay here with us?"

Allison's eyes narrowed at him.

"Hear me out." Colt raised his hands to stop her from voicing a rejection of his idea. "Jace could live here during the school year and then come to you for some holidays and part of the summer. Lots of parents work their shared custody out that way."

She scoffed. "You have no better control over Jace than I do."

Caitlyn stepped out through the screen door onto the porch. "Sorry to intrude, but I inadvertently heard the last part of your conversation." She crossed the deck and leaned against the railing. "Jace is going through a rough patch right now, but parenting isn't really about controlling him as much as it is about guiding him through the hard times. Here's the thing..." She absently caressed her still flat belly. "I'll be home now until after this little one is born. I won't be doing anything more than research, computer searches, and admin work until after the birth, and I'll be doing all of that from right here at home. So, Jace would have at least one adult around all the time. Plus, I think a little brother or sister might have a settling effect on him."

Allison returned her gaze to the yard and Jace, whom Storm had knocked over and whose face he was licking amid giggles, with Renegade barking enthusiastically at the game. A small, sad smile graced her mouth. "Are you sure you want that much responsibility?"

Colt's heart leapt at the question, but he forced himself to remain calm. His eyes darted to Caitlyn and then back to Allison. "I'm absolutely certain. *We're* certain. I know we can work this out."

Allison nodded. Colt and Caitlyn met each other's gaze. All manner of excitement and joy sparked in their eyes.

"Fine. I'll have my attorney contact you." Allison gathered her purse in her lap.

"Good. I'll expect his call. Hey, do you mind if Jace stays here for dinner tonight? I'll run him back to your house in time for bed."

"I suppose." Allison stood and smoothed her slacks. "I'll see you around eight then?"

32

It had been a long day, and Caitlyn had made her mom's comfort-food recipe of chicken and dumplings for dinner that the German side of her family had passed down for generations. Colt and she sat next to each other on the leather couch. A cozy, crackling fire warmed the room as they ate their meal from large crockery bowls.

"It's good to have everyone home." Colt put an arm around Caitlyn and pulled her close. She leaned into her husband's solid chest and sighed with contentment. Renegade and Storm had curled up together on the hearthrug, snoring softly.

Jace knelt at the end of the coffee table, gobbling down his second helping of dumplings. "I'm so hungry. I could eat five bowls full of this stuff."

Caitlyn grinned. "You're probably growing again. Eat up. There's plenty."

Colt took his and Caitlyn's empty bowls to the kitchen and rinsed them. When he returned, he sat on the edge of the couch and propped his elbows on his knees. "Jace, we need to talk to you about something."

Jace's shoulders drooped. "I know. You're going to ground me for a month, aren't you?"

Colt chuckled. "No. I'm not going to ground you at all. I think you've learned your lesson. I need to talk to you about your mom. I think you know she wants to move back to Missouri."

"Yeah, but Dad! Please don't let her take me there! I don't want to go!"

Colt held up a hand to calm his son. "You're not going. At least not now. Your mom and I talked about it, and we both think it would be best if you live here with me and Caitlyn during the school year and then you can spend the summers in Missouri with your mom." Jace's blond brows crunched together, and he shoved his bowl away. He looked so much like Colt when he got angry that Caitlyn had to bite down on a grin.

Facing Jace, she leaned forward. "Don't you like that idea?"

"I like the part where I get to stay here during school, but I don't want to go to Missouri in the summer. That's when I get to spend the most time on the ranch with Uncle Dylan. And what about 4H?"

Caitlyn reached for his hand. "I know you really like to be on the ranch. I'm sure we can work something out with your mom, but she wants to have time with you too."

Jace stared at the fire, deep in thought. "Maybe I could stay with her at Christmas and over spring break but only for a couple of weeks in the summer."

Colt pressed his hands against his knees. "It's possible we could work something like that out. I'll talk with your mom. I know she wants what's best for you, just like Caitlyn and I do." He stood. "But for now, how about some ice cream?"

"Yeah!" Jace stuffed his last dumpling in his mouth and took his bowl to the sink.

Colt dished out the mint chocolate chip. "Listen, buddy. I have a little more that I want to say about the past couple of weeks."

Jace dropped into a dining room chair. "I knew it."

"What happened is a big deal. You ditched class and ran away; both are serious actions that had dangerous consequences. You want to jump way ahead of where you are, thinking you can become a ranch hand before you've even finished middle school."

"I know." Jace folded his arms on the table and propped his chin on them.

Colt handed him a bowl of ice cream and then sat across from him. "I get that you want to be an adult. But if you leapfrog over high school, you'll miss out on some of the best times of your life. At this point, you still need parents, and you're lucky because you have three of them who love you very much. If you have a problem, then you need to talk to one of us about it. Running away never solves anything."

Caitlyn sat next to Jace. "And you're also fortunate because you get to grow up working on the ranch. Most kids never get a chance to do that. But there is so much to learn, and it takes a lifetime to absorb it. That's how Dylan did it, and Grandpa John too. There aren't any shortcuts, and when you try to skip ahead, you only cheat yourself."

"I guess." Jace sighed. "It's just that when I'm on the ranch, I'm trusted to do real work that matters. At school, my teacher treats me like I'm just a dumb kid."

Colt brushed his hand across the top of Jace's head. "You have to earn respect, Jace. That's as true at school as it is at the ranch. You listen and work hard for Uncle Dylan, and you've built his trust. What if you gave that same effort to your teacher? I bet things would change."

"Maybe." Jace perked up when Storm rested his chin on Jace's knee. "I'll try."

"Good. Now eat up. I promised to have you back to your mom's tonight by eight." Colt smiled at Caitlyn over Jace's head—his expression sparkled with innuendo.

33

The house was quiet without Jace. He'd gone to his mom's place the night before, which was nice because it gave Caitlyn and Colt a chance to reconnect and spend some time alone together. As she'd expected, Colt was seriously angry when she confessed that she'd been caught up in an explosion, but there wasn't much he could do since she and the baby were both fine. He'd asked her to re-state her promise to stay home until after their little one was born.

That morning, Caitlyn was up with the sun, and she pulled on one of Colt's flannel button-downs. She slid her feet into deerskin slippers to protect her toes from the cold, hard wooden floors as the fall temperatures leaned toward winter. She padded out to the kitchen to let the dogs out and make coffee—a pot for Colt and a decaf Keurig pod for herself. She didn't hear Colt come up behind her, but when he slid his arms around her waist and pulled her back to his warm chest, she knew she was home.

"Good morning." His breath and early whiskers tickled her ear, eliciting a giggle.

Grinning, Caitlyn turned within the circle of his embrace and threaded her fingers through the hair at his temples. "Good morning to you, too." She rose on her toes to kiss him. The previous night's passion flared once again. Coffee could wait.

Later, after a breakfast of almond-flavored French toast and perfectly crisp bacon, Caitlyn dressed for the day. She fed the dogs and took them out to play while Colt finished tidying up the kitchen. Renegade and Storm chased a tennis ball—racing to see who would get to it first. Their panting left puffs of steam floating behind them. Ren always won the race, but Storm—impossible to discourage—kept trying. Both dogs stopped their game at once and stared up the drive, hearing tires on the road before Caitlyn even noticed them. Her K9 vehicle, followed by an identical version of the same car, nosed their way toward the cabin.

"Colt!" Caitlyn called. "Logan and Addison are here!" She called the dogs so they wouldn't get in the way of the cars and waited for her brother and his wife to park and get out. Colt stepped onto the porch wiping his hands on a tea towel before holding up his hand in greeting.

Caitlyn hugged them both. "You guys made great time. I didn't expect you before lunch."

Colt jogged down the front steps as Gunner bounded out of Logan's Explorer and bolted toward Renegade and Storm. Laughing at the dogs, Colt kissed Addison's cheek and gripped Logan's hand, pulling him into a solid man-hug that included a sound patting of each other's backs. "Do you guys want breakfast? There's plenty left."

"Just coffee, if you have any. We stopped earlier to eat at an all-night diner in Gillette."

Colt bobbed his head. "Coming right up."

Logan tossed Caitlyn's key fob across the yard to her, and Caitlyn caught the keys one-handed. "Thanks again, Logan. I know it was a long drive."

"No problem. You needed to be home with your family. Besides, it'll be good to see Mom and Dad. We haven't been up here since our wedding."

Colt carried out a tray with four steaming mugs. "You guys want to sit on the porch?"

Addison led the way. "Absolutely. It's a little chilly out, but it's nice to have some fresh air." She reached for her coffee and took a long sip. Sighing with pleasure, she continued Logan's thought, "We also can't wait to see little Rose. I bet she's grown a ton already."

"Decaf for you." Colt handed Caitlyn her cup. "Yeah, she's adorable, and she keeps Dylan on his toes, that's for sure." Caitlyn accepted the mug and tried not to grimace when she sipped the weaker version of her favorite drink.

Logan laughed. "I'm looking forward to watching Dylan's gruff stoicism melt around his little girl." He sat on the porch rail and took several sips before he filled Colt and her in on the details of the terrorist plot in Denver. "The men Caitlyn and I caught at Centennial Airport were definitely working with that radical group from Westcliffe. Their ultimate goal was to murder Senator Hyatt as a last-ditch effort to stop him from building a ski resort in that area."

"Hyatt told me he wanted to develop a resort that would rival Vail." Caitlyn stirred cream into her coffee and then licked her spoon.

"Right. The radical group's secondary goal was to shut down DIA, creating a massive terror attack in the middle of the country that would cause fear in the traveling public and gain attention for their cause. The added benefit would have been to keep people from wanting to travel to or move to Colorado."

Colt raised his cup in cheers. "Sounds like you guys saved thousands of lives. Good work." The other three lifted their mugs and clanked them together.

Logan crossed his ankles. "Thank heavens you guys found Jace safe and sound."

Colt glanced at Caitlyn before he answered. "Yeah, but he'd been roughed up quite a bit." He joined Logan on the rail, leaving the cushioned seats for the women. "I'm just thankful Catie and Ren came home when they did. We never would have found Jace without them." Colt's blue-green eyes were filled with love and gratitude when they met hers, and Caitlyn's cheeks flushed.

Changing the subject, she asked, "Logan, are you guys staying the night at the ranch, then?"

"Yeah, we promised Mom we'd come for dinner and that means an overnight, too." Logan leaned against the corner post. "I talked to Burke Cameron this morning. He said the investigation is ongoing and that they haven't apprehended Ted Marrin, the leader of the Sovereign Earth Alliance, yet. Addy and I are joining Cameron's team this afternoon when they search the mine tunnels.

He told me there are two cabins on the mountain—not just the one."

Colt nodded. "That's what the map says, but I don't remember there being a second structure, do you?"

"No, but it's been years since I've been up there. You guys ought to come up to the high country with us. The more eyes, the better. We're flying up in the ATF helicopter."

Caitlyn and Colt agreed to go along, and leaving all the dogs with her brother, they went inside to get dressed.

AFTER LUNCH, they met Burke and his team at the medical clinic's helipad. The various law enforcement personnel climbed into the ATF's Black Hawk and strapped in for the flight. The chopper pilot spoke to them over the intercom. "I may not be able to set this bird down up there. Is everyone okay with rappelling?" All passengers inside affirmed the plan. "And what about the dogs?"

Logan glanced at Caitlyn, and she gave him a thumbs up. "Both Gunner and Renegade are qualified and experienced in HRST." Colt canted his head, looking confused, and Logan explained. "Helicopter Rope Suspension Techniques."

"Roger that." The pilot flipped several switches, and the rotors spooled up. "Prepare for takeoff." They lifted off and swooped over Moose Creek. Before long they were hovering over high rocky mountains, searching for a place to land. But the pilot had been correct in his early assessment. The terrain was too steep and rugged to land, so the agents prepared their harnesses to rappel.

"I've got a visual on the two cabins." The copilot pointed out his window. "And check out that cave. Is that the abandoned mine?"

Everyone turned to look out the windows, and Colt shook his head. "No. The mine is closer to the lower cabin. I haven't seen that cave entrance before. Have you, Logan?"

"No, we would have been all over that as kids if we'd have known it was there. Let's check it out now."

Caitlyn and Logan attached their dog's protective vests to their own harnesses with carabiners and waited for the others to lower themselves down first. Caitlyn and Renegade clipped onto the long rope. She leaned back, letting Renegade's weight settle against her and allowed the rope to slide through the rappelling gear at a steady pace. They were on the rocky ground seconds before Logan and Gunner landed beside them.

As soon as they released their clips, the Black Hawk crew retracted the dangling ropes and flew away. The dogs led the team to the upper building marked on the map. It wasn't much more than a glorified shack hastily slapped together with splintering gray plywood. Logan made quick work of the padlock that held the door closed. Inside the tiny room, they found a nylon pack with some clothes stuffed inside resting on a cot. A simple wooden table was pushed into the corner and held a propane-powered hotplate with a blue tin coffeepot sitting on top.

"Not much to see in here." Logan stepped outside to allow others entry. "Somebody check that pack for an ID."

Colt peered inside over Caitlyn's shoulder as she riffled through the bag. "Nothing exciting in there. Let's go investigate that cave."

The team left two ATF agents behind to complete a thorough check of the cabin while the rest of the them hiked up to the cave entrance they had seen from the helicopter. The opening was a tall, narrow space between two slabs of marble. They had to enter single-file, stepping sideways to squeeze through. Once inside, the cavern opened up enough for Caitlyn, Colt, Logan, Addison, and Burke to stand closely together. The dogs squeezed in and stood by their feet. Caitlyn unclipped a Maglite from her utility belt and shone it along the stone walls and down a lone dark tunnel that led deeper into the mountain.

"There's only about three feet of clearance in that passage. Looks like if we want to investigate, we'll have to crawl through to see where it goes."

Logan turned on his flashlight, too. "Let's do it." He crawled into the tunnel with Gunner on his heels.

"Right behind you." Colt dropped to his hands and knees.

Caitlyn peered over the men into the dark passage. "How far does it go?"

"I'm not sure." Logan sent his beam into the endless blackness.

"Logan, wait. Ren and I are coming, too. Take this."

Caitlyn handed him the end of a climbing rope she had attached to her pack. "Tie this to your belt so we don't lose our way back." Before she followed her husband and brother, she turned to Addison and Burke. "You guys stay here in case we get into any trouble."

34

Logan led the way with Gunner right behind him. Then came Colt, Caitlyn, and Renegade bringing up the rear. As they crawled deeper, the air in the narrow passage became dense. The granite walls were damp and cold. Caitlyn sensed the massive weight of the mountain pressing down around them.

"Do you guys think this is a natural cave, or part of the mine?" Her voice bounced off the stone.

Logan crawled on. "Natural, I think. There aren't any beams or structures holding up the ceiling and walls." No sooner had he said the words when his hand struck a plank on the floor. He put his weight on it and the old board snapped. The broken wood fell. Rocks tumbled downward into an abyss, and Logan, losing his balance, fell with them.

Caitlyn screamed, and Colt lunged forward, grabbing hold of Logan's boots seconds before they lost him in a hole of unknown depth. Logan's flashlight clattered down, bouncing again and again, never landing. The darkness swallowed the light.

"I've got you, Logan," Colt grunted, but together, they slid forward with nothing to anchor themselves on.

Caitlyn's heart careened against her chest wall like a jackhammer. Bracing herself against a rough section of the wall, she took hold of Colt's legs. "Hang on, Colt! I've got ahold of the rope tied to Logan's waist. I think we can use it to pull him up." She looped the length around her hips and leveraging herself against the stone, she pushed with all her might.

Logan called out. "There's a ledge. I think I can hold myself up long enough for you to get a better hold."

"Okay, good. Let's go on the count of three." Colt counted, and together the three of them strained. When Logan's hips surfaced, Gunner clamped down on his partner's belt and helped to pull him the rest of the way to safety.

Logan skuttled away from the hole and pressed his head back against the frigid stone wall. "Holy shit! That was close. You guys saved my life." He buried his fingers in Gunner's fur and hugged him.

"You should go back." Caitlyn stared at her brother's profile highlighted in her single beam. He'd scraped his forehead, and a trickle of blood ran down the side of his face. "To make sure you're alright."

"No way. I'm not letting you two go through this tunnel without me. One for all and all for one, right?"

Caitlyn shook her head and gave him a reluctant grin at the phrase they used to shout as children whenever they ran off on another grand adventure. "Are you sure you're able to continue?"

"As soon as my pulse settles down, I will be."

The hole Logan had fallen in was only a couple of feet wide—an easy span to traverse if you knew where it was. So, they took turns maneuvering over the chasm and continued down the narrow tunnel. The tight space gradually opened to a larger cavern, and Caitlyn shone her light around the stone room, gauging the size of it to be about ten feet by ten feet. They could finally stand.

A rumbling noise came from deeper inside the mountain. It grew louder.

"What is that?" Caitlyn aimed her beam toward the noise. "It sounds like a freight train."

Colt's eyes opened wide. "Turn around and cover your heads!" he yelled as he dropped to his knees. Bending his face to the floor, he held his hands over his ears.

Caitlyn covered Renegade with her body and threw an arm over her head seconds before thousands of wings flapped over and around her. Claws scraped her bare skin and caught in her hair. Bats! Their little winged bodies buffeted her from all sides for minutes on end. A primal shudder coursed through her body. She held her breath so she wouldn't scream, waiting for the onslaught to end.

When it quieted, Colt called out, "Catie, are you okay?"

She had dropped her flashlight, and the light went out. No one could see anything. "I'm okay. But that was awful. Will they come back?" Caitlyn felt around on the ground for her Maglite. Finding it, her fingers curled around the cold metal barrel, and she turned it on as soon as her fingers located the switch. Along with the light, relief poured through her.

"No, they'll fly out the opening and hide in the trees. They probably won't return until nighttime." Colt scooted over to her and pulled her close. "Are you sure you're okay?"

"Just creeped out. Did you say, *probably*?" Caitlyn grimaced and Renegade licked her cheek. "Do we go further down the tunnel, or do we get out of here?"

Logan and Gunner moved closer to them. "Hand me your flashlight."

Caitlyn passed it to him, and he sent the light across the floor. A dark lump huddled at the base of the wall next to a stack of wooden boxes. "Is that a body?"

Logan crept toward the soft form and rolled it over. "Colt, could this be your missing man?"

"Is he dead?" Colt crawled across the dirt floor and knelt next to Logan.

Logan felt the man's neck for a pulse. "I think he's still alive. Barely. But his body temperature is dangerously low. We need to get him out of here and to the hospital as soon as possible." He raised the beam and caught the shapes of two stacks of wooden crates lined up against the wall. "Wonder what we'll find in these. Hold this for me." Logan passed the flashlight back to Caitlyn.

She held the beam as steady as she could while she removed her jacket and lay it across the unconscious man. Colt and Logan pried the lid off one of the containers. Inside, they found a stack of automatic rifles. The three law enforcement officers stared at each other without commenting. Logan opened another. "Handguns." He and Colt moved the top boxes to the floor so they could look inside the others. Upon closer inspection, they discovered a large selection of guns. "These weapons look new. No doubt there meant for the black market."

Caitlyn crawled to a metal box nestled on the side of one of the stacks and wrestled the lid open. "Logan." Her face stiffened. "This container is packed with bricks of C4." She sat back on her heels. "How did someone get all of this in here? The tunnel is too narrow."

"It's a good question. One we'll ask our recovery team to figure out. We can send them back for it and get all this stuff to the lab, but first we have to get this man some medical care."

"Catie." Colt rested his hand on Caitlyn's shoulder. "Turn off the light for a second."

"Why?"

"Just turn it off for just a minute."

Caitlyn did as he asked, and the stone room was instantly swathed in black. The space was so dark she couldn't see the edge of anything. Gradually her eyes adjusted, and she picked up the slightest hint of light. "Is that another passage?"

"I think so." Colt's fingers felt their way down her arm and took the flashlight from her. He clicked it on and aimed the beam toward the glow they had seen. "Yeah, look. There's another tunnel, bigger than this one. We can probably walk out if we duck our heads. I bet this passage leads to another way out."

This time, Caitlyn led the way with Renegade while Logan and Colt carried the injured man toward the light. Gunner brought up the tail end. The air gradually became easier to breathe, and the diffused light around them increased.

Before long, Caitlyn halted the procession at the precipice of another hole in the floor of the tunnel. They found themselves looking down into a large empty space. The light from outside was much brighter here.

Colt and Logan set the man on the floor, and lying on their stomachs, assessed the situation below. Colt pushed himself up to his haunches. "That's a large cavern down there. It looks like it's about a ten-foot drop to the bottom, though. I can ease myself down and then help Catie. Logan, can you lower the man down to us?"

"Yeah, sounds good." Logan pulled the length of rope coiling it until he came to the end of it. "We can use this rope to stabilize our John Doe as we pass him down."

Colt rolled to his belly and scooted his legs over the edge. He hung as far down as he could before letting go and dropping to the ground below. Caitlyn repeated his maneuver, but Logan held her hands and lowered her far enough for Colt to grasp hold of her legs. She slid down his body until her feet hit the floor.

She looked up at Logan. "Send the dogs next. Colt and I can catch them."

Once the dogs were safely down, Logan tied the rope around the man's body, tightening it under his arms. "Okay, I've got a good foot hold, so I'm going to start lowering this guy down to you."

"I'm ready." Colt raised his hands to receive the large unconscious man. Caitlyn did her best to bear some of the dead weight descending from above. Together, she and Colt caught his feet and legs, and eased him gently onto the floor.

Caitlyn checked the man's pulse again. "Thready, but present."

Logan lowered himself down and once they were all standing in the sunlit cavern, they recognized where they were. As kids, they'd played in this part of the mine shaft many times. Colt jogged up a short tunnel to the entrance. "This is the section of the cave where Wes and Izzy found the explosives, the journal, maps, and the blueprint."

"I'm starting to believe our two cases are connected somehow, but I can't string it together." Caitlyn chewed her lip.

Logan stared up at the hole in the ceiling they had all dropped down from. "I don't see how they could be. At least not in the way you might think."

Caitlyn narrowed her eyes and cocked her head. "But it's too much of a coincidence having two criminal factions running around up here at the same time."

"True, but I tend to agree with Logan." Colt scrolled through his phone for the photos Izzy had taken when they discovered the items in the cave. "I wonder if Sandlewood stumbled upon the loot and was bringing some of what he discovered out with him when Dray and his crew spotted him."

"Could Dray be the weapons dealer?" Logan adjusted the coat on the frozen man and rubbed his arms for warmth. "He could have grabbed Sandlewood and dragged him to the cabin."

Caitlyn stamped her feet to warm them. "If you hadn't

found the film student when you did, they probably would have left them both up here to die in these tunnels." She chewed on her lip. "I have no doubt the weapons belong to the Sovereign Earth Alliance, but it seems like too much—Mason Dray is trying to buy up the private land around here at the same time as the Sovereign Earth Alliance is stashing weapons in these caves."

"It is strange, for sure, but Dray building a hundred houses would never come close to making the kind of money he would make smuggling guns and explosives." Logan brushed dirt off his pants. "And why would he want the extra attention? Honestly, I think there are two criminal factions here at one time. One, the Alliance who wanted to deal in weapons and explosives from the upper cave and two, a sleazy developer who hid Molotov cocktail components in the lower mineshaft."

"Yeah, Dray's a Class A jerk, but he's not the type to run guns," agreed Colt. "And finding the blueprint of DIA hidden in the depths of the tunnels, makes it highly probable that the weapons and C4 stash is connected to the bombings in Denver."

Logan stripped off his outer jacket and added it to the extra clothing already covering the freezing man who was barely clinging to life. "The lab can tell us if the C4 is from the same batch as that from Denver. Get Cameron on the phone. We need Flight for Life and have him tell the Black Hawk to bring an investigative team up here. And Addison will personally want to supervise the removal of those crates of C4.

35

William Logan called Addison, Colt used his sat phone to contact the Moose Creek Emergency Clinic. After identifying himself, he asked if Doctor Kennedy was at the hospital.

The receptionist hemmed. "I think he's here some-where unless he left for lunch. Let me page him. Will you hold a sec, Sheriff?"

"Yes, but please hurry. This is an emergency." Colt swallowed his frustration. "Catie, can you look again for anything that might identify this man? I think he's our missing hunter, but I need to be certain."

"Sure." Caitlyn patted the man's pants pockets and moved up his body to check his coat. "Nothing."

"Okay, take his picture. As soon as I have cell cover-age, I'll send it to Wes. He can compare the image with the photo Mrs. Sandlewood emailed to us. Until then—" Colt turned back to his phone. "Yes, I'm still here."

"Please hold for Doctor Kennedy."

"Colt? What's happened? My nurse said there's been an emergency."

"Yes. We found a man in a cave up in the high country. His heart is beating, but he is unresponsive. His body temperature seems lower than it should be. He has some cuts and possibly animal bites on his arms along with bruising and some older injuries. We've performed what basic first aid we could, but he remains unconscious. Should we be doing anything more for him than what we already are?"

"Do you think he might have hypothermia?"

"It's possible, Doc. But that's your expertise, not mine."

"How soon can you get him to the ER?"

"A helicopter is on its way. But it will still take a minimum of forty-five minutes to get him loaded up and then back down there."

"I'm concerned that he may have a head injury. I don't think it's wise to bring him here when he might need help that our little clinic isn't equipped to provide. Have the pilot fly you over to Monument Health over in Spearfish. I'll call them so they'll be prepared for your arrival. Until then, tell me, is any of the patient's clothing wet?"

Colt tapped on the phone screen. "I have you on speaker, Doc. Caitlyn and Logan are here with me."

"Good. Check for wet clothing. If so, remove it and replace it with dry fabric. You'll want to begin warming him, but not too quickly. If you heat him too fast, it can cause heart problems. Keep a close eye on his breathing and pulse. You may need to start CPR."

Caitlyn removed the two jackets they had placed over his clothes earlier and felt his shirt. It was cold and damp. "Logan, help me get this off." She unclipped her Leatherman and pulled out the knife blade. Without hesitation, she slit the man's shirt up the back. Logan lifted him higher so she could pull the cold fabric away. Logan then stripped off his own long-sleeved Under Armour shirt, and they stretched the warm shirt over the man's head before replacing their jackets around him. Colt tossed Logan his coat and buttoned his flannel shirt up to the top.

"Okay, we've changed his shirt."

"Good. See if you have any chemical heat packs in your first-aid kits. You can gently warm him but go slow. When the helicopter gets there, cover him with blankets."

The unmistakable sound of the Black Hawk echoed against the walls of the canyon. "They're here. Thanks, Blake."

"Good. Keep me informed, will you? And stay safe... all of you."

Colt glanced at Caitlyn, but she ignored the comment. "Will do."

Addison had clearly given the pilot their specific GPS coordinates. The helicopter hovered above them and lowered a gurney down to them on a rope. Colt and Logan lifted the man into the basket and strapped him in. The flight crew sent a second rope down with a harness for one of them.

"I'll going with him." Colt reached for the line. "That way I can call his wife if we determine this is Sandlewood." He tilted Caitlyn's chin up and kissed her. "I'll miss dinner at your parent's house tonight, but I promised Jace he could come to see his Uncle Logan and Aunt Addy. Can you pick him up at Allison's?"

"Of course I can. Let me know what happens and if you need me to come get you in Spearfish." She pulled him close and held tight.

He pressed his lips against the top of her head. "I will."

The rescue gurney rose from the ground, swinging slightly toward the helicopter. Colt strapped himself into the harness, and the ropes hoisted him off the mountain. By the time the crew pulled him aboard, a medic was already attending to the patient. He had covered the man with wool blankets and was setting him up with an IV.

Colt tugged on the headset that was offered to him. "We need to fly to Spearfish, South Dakota. The hospital there is waiting for us."

The helicopter had its own internet connection, and Colt hooked his phone into it. He texted Wes the photo of the man who lay unconscious before him. Seconds later, Wes messaged back.

"Yep, that's Sandlewood, alright! Way to go, Sheriff. Is he alive?"

Colt responded by filling Wes in on what happened and his plan.

"I'll call Mrs. Sandlewood as soon as we get to the hospital."

"This will wreck his daughter's wedding plans."

"Not as badly as it would have if we'd have found him dead."

"True."

When they arrived at the hospital, Colt filled the doctors in on what he knew, and the emergency staff worked quickly to stabilize Paul Sandlewood. He was taken away to the emergency room and Colt made his first phone call.

"Mrs. Sandlewood, this is Sheriff Colt Branson in Moose Creek."

"Yes, Sheriff?" The woman's voice broke. "You found him, didn't you?"

"Yes, ma'am, but don't worry. He's alive. We are at the hospital in Spearfish, South Dakota. Your husband is suffering from exposure and hypothermia. He was unconscious when we found him, but he is in good care now."

"He's alive? I was sure you were calling to tell me..." Mrs. Sandlewood burst into tears.

"Yes, he's alive, but he is in serious condition. Can you fly up here?"

"Of course," she cried. "I'll be there as soon as I can."

"I'll stay with him until you get here."

"I can't thank you enough, Sheriff. You're so kind." The woman dissolved in wracking sobs.

Finally, a younger woman got on the phone. "Sheriff, this is Stephanie Sandlewood. Thank you for calling. My dad's brother lives in Deadwood. I'll call him and have him go to the hospital to be with my dad until my mom and I can fly up. Thank you so much for all you've done."

"No problem. Please stay in touch with his progress."

"We will."

Colt murmured a quick prayer for Paul Sandlewood before he dialed Allison.

36

———

Jace rushed to finish his homework as he listened to his mom talking on the phone with his dad. She had agreed to let him go to dinner at the ranch since his Aunt and Uncle were in town. Jace couldn't believe his luck.

"Jace," His mom was off the phone. "Caitlyn will be here at five o'clock to pick you up. But you're not going unless you finish your schoolwork. Is that clear?"

"Yes, ma'am." In his rush, he messed up his math problem and had to start over. He worked harder than ever for the next hour, and by the time Caitlyn pulled into their driveway, he was putting the finishing touches on his book report.

Jace sat in the front seat of her K9 Explorer while Storm and Renegade rode together in the kennel. "Where's Dad?"

"He flew to Spearfish with a man we found inside one of the caves this afternoon. The guy was in bad shape and your dad wanted to stay with him until his family could get to the hospital."

"Will Dad be able to make it for dinner?" His stomach rumbled, and he couldn't wait for his grandma's cooking. Whatever she was making, he knew it would be great!

"I don't know for sure, but I'm not counting on it."

When they got to the ranch, Uncle Logan and Aunt Addy weren't there yet, so they had to wait. When they finally pulled up, Jace ran out the front door and launched himself off the deck at Logan who, luckily, caught him and swung him around.

"Hey, kiddo! I hear you struck out on a lone backpacking adventure. How about next time you, your dad, and I go together?"

"Really?"

"Sure. Between the two of us, we can probably teach your dad a few things." Logan set Jace on his feet.

Caitlyn's whole family sat around the long walnut table in the dining room. Jace mentally corrected the thought. *His* family. He smiled to himself and listened to the adults talk as he scooped huge bites of food into his mouth. Grandma Stella had made barbecue brisket with mashed potatoes and baked beans. There were three vegetable casseroles and her special sweet cornbread. And best of all, he'd seen two of her blue-ribbon apple pies sitting on the counter in the kitchen for dessert.

Jace was helping clear the table when his dad came in through the front door. "Looks like I missed dinner, but I'm just in time for dessert."

Grandma Stella smiled at him. "Oh Colt, I'm so glad

you made it. And don't you worry. I made a plate and put it aside for you."

Caitlyn crossed the room and kissed his dad. Jace looked away as she took his hand and led him to the table. "I didn't think you'd make it home so soon. How is Mr. Sandlewood doing?"

"He was pretty much the same when I left. His brother drove over from Deadwood, so I felt I could leave. I caught a ride over to Moose Creek with an EMT who commutes from Carlile. He dropped me at the office where I left my Jeep." His dad and Caitlyn sat together at the table. "McKenzie, how is that stray dog we found up at the mine doing?"

"He's great. With Doctor Moore's help, he's on his way back to a healthy weight, and we were able to adopt him out to an older couple."

"So, he wasn't chipped?"

"No, and we put a notice in the local paper, but never heard anything."

"He probably got separated from his people when they were camping in the national park. Is the adoptive couple anyone we know?"

"Maybe. They're a local ranch family. Do you know Cecil and Sheri Colwell? They've been looking for a dog to be a companion and who would also alert them to any strangers on their property."

Jace's dad smiled. "Theirs was one of the ranches that Mason Dray's goons vandalized in hopes of scaring them into selling. They burned down his workshop by throwing a Molotov cocktail through the window. The Colwell's will be perfect dog owners, and it will be good for all involved." He pushed his chair back from the table. "Jace, I have something for you."

Jace reluctantly set his stack of plates down. He had wanted to finish clearing up so he could dig into a big piece of pie. "Yeah?"

His dad reached into his shirt pocket and pulled out a thin silver device. "Now, this cell can only call or text me, Caitlyn, your mom, and your grandparents, and it doesn't connect to the internet. But I think you deserve a new phone since the one you had got ruined, and it wasn't your fault. In fact, I wanted to tell you that the video you texted to Uncle Dylan came through before those men smashed your phone. We will be able to use the film as evidence of Dray's dishonest business practices and his assault on you. That was levelheaded thinking on your part, and I'm very proud of you."

"Thanks, Dad!" Jace was happy to get a new phone, but he was even more excited that his video would help keep the bad guys in jail. And the way his dad looked at him meant everything. Jace hugged him around the neck as hard as he could.

"You're welcome, son," his dad said, then he spoke to everyone at the table. "Now, we have a family announcement to make." The talking stopped and all eyes turned toward Jace's dad. "Allison is moving back to Missouri and has agreed to let Jace stay here with us during the school year." A happy shout went up and the whole family started talking at once, making plans and congratulating him. Jace's body warmed. He was perfectly happy in the middle of this loud and loving home where he belonged. He was a little worried he'd end up missing a lot of 4H, but he wouldn't think too hard about that for now.

"Do you think Dylan will implode that old mine?" Caitlyn scraped her fork across her pie plate, making sure to get every last crumb. She, Colt, Logan and Addison had carried their pie plates down to the arena to eat while they watched Jace ride his horse.

"The mine is on federal property, so unless the government orders it to be done, I doubt it will be." Logan grinned. "Besides, it's a great hideout, right, Colt? We should take Jace up there and show it to him."

Colt chuffed. "I'd rather he stayed away from that hole you almost fell in. Besides, I think I've had enough spelunking for the time being."

Addison set her empty plate on top of Caitlyn's and then rubbed her sister-in-law's shoulders. "So, you're home for a while now, huh?"

"Yep. I'm actually looking forward to being around here more." She winked at her stepson as he rode by, and he smiled in return. "Life is going to be a lot quieter until our baby is born. Then, from what I hear, I'll probably want to get back to work so I can rest!"

Colt took the stack of plates and kissed her on the cheek. "I, for one, am glad you'll be home where I can keep an eye on you. You were in a lot more danger down in Denver than you let on."

Caitlyn smiled up at him. He didn't even know half of it. She'd tell him the rest, but not for a few days. Not until they had more time and distance from the events. Renegade, who had been sniffing around everyone's feet, sat down and barked. Laughing, Colt set three plates on the ground for the dogs to clean up. Caitlyn shook her head. How was she going to keep Ren disciplined with Colt giving him treats all the time?

Her phone rang. "Sorry guys, I have to take this." Colt gave her a hard look. "Don't look at me like that. It's Dirk." She stepped away to speak to her US Marshal mentor and friend, Dirk Sterling.

"Hey, kiddo. I heard about your mission in Denver. Glad you came out of that okay."

"Thanks. I'm just glad we caught the terrorists before they hurt more innocent people."

"I also hear you're going to be chained to your computer for several months."

"That's the cold, hard truth," she groaned.

"Well, I'm searching for a former Army Ranger turned contract killer. Can I count on you for some admin help?"

"Of course."

"I knew you'd want in. Teresa will call you next week and share what she has so far. How long are you taking for maternity leave after your baby is born?"

"I have the usual six weeks. After that, I'll have to figure out how to be a working mom. I'll have two kids, you know."

"That's true, and I have no doubt you'll figure it out."

Caitlyn chewed on her bottom lip. *I hope so. Lots of women do it. I'm sure I can too.*

"And since you're going to be home, I need to ask you another small favor..."

~ The End ~

THANK YOU FOR READING **DETONATE**. I hope you enjoyed thrilling adventures with Caitlyn and Renegade and some of our favorite characters from books past!

IF YOU LOVED READING **DETONATE**, Book 9 in the Tin Star K9 Series, I would be most honored if you would please take a moment to write a quick review.

Review DETONATE

Thank you so much!

***

The Adventure Continues!
Next!
Book 10 in the Tin Star K9 Series

SURVIVAL

Motherhood hasn't dulled Caitlyn Reed's edge—it's sharpened her resolve. The US Deputy Marshal and her loyal K9, Renegade, are itching to return to the field despite her husband Colt's insistence on caution. So, when Search and Rescue calls, Caitlyn seizes the chance to prove she can balance diapers and danger. But what begins as a simple mountain rescue spirals into a fight for survival, forcing Caitlyn to face the ultimate test: can she protect herself and make it home to the family who needs her most?

Order your copy of SURVIVAL today!

For free books and to join my reader group, please visit my website: Jodi-Burnett.com

ACKNOWLEDGMENTS

First, and always, I thank God for blessing me with a vivid imagination, work I love, and for the inspiration with which to do it. A creative calling isn't always easy, but it is always rich. Thank You, Lord.

I gave myself more time to write Detonate and re-realized I do better with hard deadlines! I might not have finished if it wasn't for the continual encouragement of my husband, Chris, and my friend Karen who frequently asked how my book was coming along. Thanks for the accountability, you two!

I'd also like to thank the members of my writer's mastermind group, affectionately known as "Kool-Aid." Corinne and Dominika, if it weren't for you two helping me with the business and technical side of writing, I'd be lost in the weeds forever!

As always, I am eternally grateful for Kae, my editor, my Beta Reading team, and my ARC team. As they say, "It takes a village." And that is so true with a book. I'd never publish anything without all of you!

I could not do any of this without the support and encouragement of my family. Writing can be such a solo venture. Thanks for pulling me out of my cave and loving me through the rough spots. I cherish the inside jokes, all the music and sports, and most especially the way we love each other. My cup overflows. You are my deepest blessing.

Most of all, I want to thank Chris. It was you who came up with the idea for Caitlyn and Logan working together and I had such fun bringing old characters/friends back to life in this book. Thanks for the easy way you encourage me without any pressure. You're the best! I love you so much!

MARSHAL

JUSTICE

BLOODLINE

TRIFECTA

<u>QUALIFIED (Novella)</u>

<u>TRIALS</u>

<u>SPEC OPS</u>

<u>DETONATE</u>

-

<u>US Marshal Dirk Sterling Trilogy</u>

FORGED (Free Prequel)

EXTRACTION

CORRUPTION

<u>REDEMPTION</u>

<u>WITSEC</u>

ALSO BY JODI BURNETT

For all book formats

Go to Jodi-Burnett.com

Flint River Series

Run For The Hills

Hidden In The Hills

Danger In The Hills

A Flint River Christmas (Free Epilogue)

A Flint River Cookbook (Free Book)

FBI-K9 Thriller Series

Baxter K9 Hero (Free Prequel)

Avenging Adam

Body Count

Concealed Cargo

Mile High Mayhem

Tin Star K9 Series

RENEGADE

MAVERICK

CARNIVAL (Novella)